"Who says you date my brother?"

Andrea stiffened perceptibly. "Why? Don't you think I'm Robert's type?"

"I wonder if you're going to tell me that you love him."

She met his eyes then, forcing herself to hold his stare. "I'm going to marry him, Jason," she said firmly. "Just as your father wanted."

"I used to know what you wanted, Andy. You wanted a man who was capable of setting the stars on fire when he touched you." Jason's voice was far more threatening than the smile that edged up the corners of his mouth. "It offends my sense of romance to see you settle for less than you could have. If you love my brother enough to marry him, the least I can do is make him jealous—bring him to his knees for you." His words tore at her jumpy nerves. "Consider it a wedding present."

SHARRON COHEN is happily married. In fact, her husband is the role-model for all her heroes, although, she says candidly, he doesn't dress as well as most of them. This American author from Massachusetts, in addition to her romance novel writing, has written a local newspaper column about children and has done short story writing for a magazine.

Odd Man Out

Sharron Cohen

Harlequin Books

TORONTO • NEW YORK • LONDON
AMSTERDAM • PARIS • SYDNEY • HAMBURG
STOCKHOLM • ATHENS • TOKYO • MILAN

Original hardcover edition published in 1986
by Mills & Boon Limited

ISBN 0-373-2839-3

Harlequin Romance first edition June 1987

Printed in U.S.A.

CHAPTER ONE

'I'M Creighton Dorning's son.' The man at the door announced that fact as if he were defying Andrea to contradict him. 'I'm here about his will.'

Jason! Andrea McKinley met his brown-eyed stare with such surprise she was momentarily speechless. The last time she had seen him she had been as hopelessly in love with him as any fifteen-year-old girl could be. But that had been ten years ago, and now he didn't recognise the woman she had become. He gave her only a cursory glance before his lips thinned with impatience. 'May I come in?' he asked more clearly when she didn't move.

'Yes, of course,' she said, stepping back to gesture him into the hallway. 'I'm sorry we couldn't reach you in time for the funeral,' she apologised, giving him a feeble smile he didn't bother to return. 'Your father's death came as such a shock we weren't prepared for everything we had to do. Well,' she rubbed her hands against her hips in a nervous gesture when he didn't answer, 'you'll want to see your brother,' she ended hopefully.

'I wouldn't lay a bet on it.'

He hadn't changed very much, Andrea thought, casting a quick, sidelong glance at the contours of his tanned, taut face. He was older now, of course, and there were creases at the corners of his eyes that made her think his face was more accustomed to a smile than to the tense impatience that had settled there right now. But she would have recognised him if she'd seen him in a crowd.

He's in the library,' she said, leading the way along the hall to an open door at the end. 'We're waiting for your father's lawyer. Robert,' she announced, 'your brother is here to see you.'

'Jason?' Robert looked up from his father's desk. 'I didn't know you were coming.' He rose and stepped around the desk with his hand extended for a greeting. 'How are you, Jason? It's been a long time. What has it been? Six years? Seven?'

Jason ignored the hand, and Robert withdrew it with aggrieved embarrassment. 'I'm sorry we couldn't reach you in time for Father's funeral,' he apologised. 'I called your old address, but the phone had been disconnected.'

'Nice of you to try so hard. Under the circumstances.'

Robert's face stiffened into a mask of anger, but he didn't answer Jason's sarcastic accusation. Andrea suspected it was true. He could have found his brother in time for the funeral if he had wanted to, but gossip had always followed Jason Dorning and Robert had wanted to bury his father with as little of that as possible.

'Why don't you sit down?' suggested Robert coolly, gesturing to a chair beside the window. 'The lawyer will be here in a few minutes. If you don't mind, I have a great deal of work to do,' he continued evenly. He didn't wait for Jason's permission before he slipped on his reading glasses and studied the papers that were spread in front of him.

And that was that, Andrea thought, studying the two sullen half-brothers. They hadn't seen each other in ten years, and they couldn't manage anything more pleasant than muttered invitations to sit down.

Robert was the older of the two, and by far the handsomer, with brown hair and a finely featured face. He looked a great deal like Elizabeth Dorning, his socialite mother, who had died several years before.

Jason looked like his father. His face was fuller than his brother's, and quite a bit more tanned, with wide, thin lips that had always given Andrea the impression of a primitive sensuality even before she was old enough to understand the gossip that surrounded the conditions of his birth.

A love-child, the Dorning housekeeper had called him euphemistically, but the bits of gossip that trailed off whenever Andrea had come into the room had made her wonder how much love had been involved. Roberta Carter had been a receptionist at Creighton Dorning's office, a woman of passing prettiness and a more than willing nature where her employer was concerned. Maybe the conception of a child was as much of an unpleasant shock to her as it had been to Creighton Dorning, or perhaps the gossips were correct in assuming that she had planned the pregnancy as a way of holding a man who was quickly losing interest.

She hadn't held Creighton Dorning with a child, but he had never refused to face up to the truth. Jason was his son. He had even brought him to live at the Dorning estate for a brief time, but the reception he had received from Elizabeth Dorning and his half-brother had been far from warm and friendly. That had been the year Andrea was fifteen.

'What is this note about?'

'I beg your pardon?' Andrea recalled herself from the haze of long-past memories. 'What did you ask me, Robert?'

'This note from Janice Pantonne.' He held a beige-coloured sheet of paper in his hand. ' "We are sorry that you cannot attend our anniversary party on Saturday, but of course we understand. It was good of Andrea to call us." '

'I told them we couldn't go because of your father's death.'

'I was planning to conduct some business with Albert Pantonne at that party.' He took off his glasses and laid them on the desk, massaging the bridge of his nose with his fingers in a weary gesture. His face showed the strain he had endured since his father's unexpected death two weeks before. There had been details of the company to attend to as well as funeral arrangements to make, but it had been the questions and the gossip that had taken the greatest toll.

'Then I'll call Janice and tell her we can attend after all,' Andrea suggested practically, taking the letter from his hand. 'It would probably do you good to get away from the office and relax, anyway.'

'Yes.' He gave her a grateful smile. 'Thank you, darling.'

Jason listened to the conversation unapologetically, then his eyes came up to meet her blue-eyed gaze. 'You're not Robert's secretary?'

'No, Mr Dorning,' she answered evenly. 'I'm not your brother's secretary.'

He stared at her with renewed interest, his sharp brown eyes moving down across her loosely-woven sweater, brown tweed skirt and leather boots, then back to her face. For just a moment there was a glimmer of bewildered recognition in his eyes, but that passed just as quickly as it had come and was replaced by a tight smile of grudging appreciation. 'Lucky Robert,' Jason murmured tersely.

It was a compliment, Andrea realised, unnerved by how much she liked it, and unnerved, too, by how unexpectedly giddy she felt under the open curiosity of Jason's stare. 'I don't suppose you remember me, Mr Dorning,' she faltered with an introduction. 'My father was . . .'. She got no further before the doorbell rang. 'Excuse me,' she apologised, feeling the warmth of the eyes that followed her as she left the room.

She was an ordinary woman, tall and long-limbed with a head of thick brown hair that she kept neatly tied into a bun at the nape of her long neck. Her eyes were a shade of blue that excited no particular attention, and her features, although pleasant enough, were completely plain. She had made the best she could of life by realising that her major virtue was a gift for being helpful rather than exciting. Still, for one short moment, Jason's openly assessing gaze had made her feel an arousing rush of exhilaration she couldn't quite explain.

'Mr Carpezzi,' Andrea greeted the elderly lawyer at the door. 'We've been waiting for you. Shall I take your coat?'

'Thank you, Andrea.' The older man slipped off his heavy overcoat and let Andrea take it from his arms. Then he gave her a second, curious glance. 'You look different today, my dear. Have you done something with your hair?'

'No,' she answered, leading the way back to the library. 'I'm the same woman I've always been.'

'Vincent Carpezzi, this is Jason Dorning,' she introduced the lawyer to the man who rose from his chair. 'He's Creighton Dorning's younger son.'

'Yes, I know. I took the liberty of contacting him because he's mentioned in the will. How do you do?' He held out his hand and Jason shook it. 'I'm glad you could be here today. Your father was very insistent that all his children be here for the playing of his will.'

'All?' Jason asked him curiously. 'Is there somebody we don't know about?' Andrea was far more interested in the way the lawyer had phrased the process of delivering the information. How did someone 'play' a will?

'Robert Dorning, Jason Dorning, and Andrea McKinley,' Vincent Carpezzi ticked off the names. 'He already considered Andrea part of the family, although he didn't live long enough to see her married to his son.'

'McKinley?' Jason turned around to meet Andrea's eyes with a burst of incredulous recognition. '*Andy*?' Surprise gave way to another emotion, one which seemed like honest pleasure at their unexpected meeting. Then his eyes swept down again, taking in the woman's body that had blossomed in the past ten years. 'The little tomboy grew up,' he murmured appreciatively. 'I'll be damned.'

'Some people have predicted that,' she responded wryly, beguiled by his open admiration. 'Can I make you a drink, Mr Dorning?'

'No.' His eyes still lingered on her face, as softly seductive as a touch, and Andrea looked away before she lost herself completely in the fathomless depths of his brown eyes.

'Can I make you a drink, Robert?' she offered helpfully. 'Your usual?'

'Yes, dear,' Robert answered distractedly, opening a cabinet to reveal a television set and a video cassette player. 'That would be nice.'

'Mr Carpezzi?'

'Rye, with a splash of water, if you would, my dear.'

When they all were settled with their drinks, Mr Carpezzi pulled the curtains across the windows and dimmed the lights. Then he pushed a button on the television panel, and the screen flickered into life.

'Vincent tells me this is legal,' Creighton Dorning announced with no preliminary greeting. The white-haired man sat behind the same rosewood desk that Robert sat at now, and stared unblinkingly into the camera. 'But just to be on the safe side, he says I have to go through all that mumbo-jumbo of identifying myself. As if you don't know who I am or what's become of me.

'All riqht.' He waved his hand impatiently. 'I, Creighton Samuel Dorning, being of sound mind, if not necessarily sound body, do declare this to be my last will and testament. Dr Winston has told me that I probably won't make it past the beginning of the year. He's got a long name for the particular kind of growth he's found, but the only thing you have to know is that I've got something in my body that's more interested in killing me than in keeping me alive. I haven't told any of you because I don't care to spend my last few months being treated like an invalid.'

Andrea couldn't help a slow, sad smile. That was exactly the way Creighton Dorning had always lived his life. He had always done exactly what he pleased.

'That's settled,' the old man muttered, pouring himself a glass of brandy and taking a sip before he set it on his desk. 'A man who's facing death spends a lot of time thinking about the disappointments in his life, and I've been thinking about mine.

'I don't know which son has disappointed me the most,' Creighton Dorning went on in a peevishly cranky voice. 'I don't have to tell you about my problems with Jason.'

'But you will,' Jason guessed, speaking to the

image on the screen.

'But I will,' the old man confirmed his son's expectation. 'Now, I'm not going to say he had a normal childhood. His mother was a damn sight less interested in him than she was in holding me. When that didn't work, she offered me full custody in exchange for fifty thousand dollars, which I was glad to pay to get him out of her hands.'

Andrea glanced across the darkened room, trying to read the emotion that flickered like a cloud across Jason Dorning's face. He wasn't as handsome as his older brother, but there was a sense of wilful power in his dark eyes and lean, tense features. Stubborn and defiant as he was now, he looked very much like his successful father.

'I sent him to the best schools in the country, intending to give him a share of the company some day. But he had the audacity to tell me he didn't want any part of me. He said he'd never take my money, and he didn't even want my name. He intended to live life on *his* terms, not mine, if you can believe that kind of foolishness.

'I'm not too thrilled with Robert, either,' Creighton continued irritably. 'I was for a while. He went to law school, and then he joined the company, just as I wanted. He's a good businessman. That's the problem,' he admitted, taking a long sip of brandy to wet his parched throat. 'The company has become an addiction for him. Never mind that we're the largest importers of produce on the east coast, he has to make more money every year. I don't think he'll ever be satisfied with what he has.

To tell the God's honest truth, he doesn't even *know* what he has.

'I'm talking about Andrea,' the old man said pointedly. 'He's been seeing her for almost a year now, and what do I have to show for it? Not a daughter-in-law. Certainly not the grandchildren I would have liked before I died. He hasn't proposed to her. I don't even think he's slept with her,' he said derisively. 'How long do you think it would have taken Jason to drag her off to bed?'

'Ten minutes,' suggested Jason, casting her a sidelong glance.

'Andrea is the only one who has never disappointed me,' the old man volunteered, his face softening into a smile as he folded his hands in front of him on the shiny rosewood surface of the desk. 'Don't you make the mistake of thinking that because her father was the chauffeur here Andrea should be happy to have you, Robert. She's *nobility*.' He said the word with such passionate intensity his voice reverberated in the air. 'And I don't mean anything about bank accounts and blood lines. It's something that a man sees with his heart when he falls in love with a woman. I've seen it well enough. I have always liked that girl. She is the one I'm going to miss the most. And she is probably the one who has suffered the most from my death. I'm truly sorry.'

Andrea gritted her teeth together to keep from bursting into tears. She had grown to love the old man, too. She was relieved he had known that.

'I wanted to say goodbye to you, Andrea,'

Creighton Dorning admitted quietly. 'But I didn't want to see you cry. Hell, I'll tell you the truth. What does it matter now?' he asked in a faltering voice. 'I didn't want you to see *me* cry. A man has to pretend to be a man, even when he's frightened.'

The tears welled up and fell across Andrea's pale cheeks, and she used her palm to quickly wipe them back.

'Enough of this morbid conversation.' Creighton Dorning quickly changed the subject. 'Andrea, my dear,' he leaned forward with a smile, 'I am leaving you the sum of twenty-five thousand dollars, plus the painting of the bathers that hangs in the living room, because you've always liked it so much.

'My son Jason professes to care about literature,' the old man went on. 'So I'm leaving him a box of my favourite books in the hope that he will read them and learn something about good writing. The box is in my bedroom, labelled with his name. Robert knows the value of business contacts, so I am leaving him my address book. I'm sure he will use it to make more money than he needs.'

'What about the company?' Robert asked sharply, staring at the screen.

The old man looked immensely pleased by the suspense. 'But what about the rest of it?' he echoed Robert's thoughts. 'I've got a house and cars and stocks, and the Dorning Import Company. All told, I'm worth about eighty-three million dollars.' Jason let out a low whistle of surprise.

'I'd like grandchildren,' the old man admitted. 'I wouldn't mind if the first boy were named after me, but since I'm soon to be dead, I'll never know. I'd like those children to be Andrea's. *Before* she dies of old age,' he added pointedly. 'To that end, here is the main provision of my will.

'My son is to inherit my entire estate on the day that he marries Andrea McKinley. Until such time as the marriage takes place, Robert may continue as acting president of Dorning Imports.

'Goodbye. And good luck to all of you.' The old man lifted his glass of brandy in a toast and smiled broadly just before the screen went blank.

There was a long moment of silence in the room, as if Creighton Dorning's powerful presence lingered there after his image faded, then, one by one, the participants broke away from their private thoughts and began to stir.

'As soon as I've attended to the most pressing company business, Andrea and I will get married,' Robert said matter-of-factly as the lawyer stood up to rewind the tape. 'That's simple enough.'

'Hm,' Jason agreed as he stood up and retrieved his heavy coat from the back of the Queen Anne chair. 'It's the fifty years after that that are going to be the tough part. Show me where the box is,' he turned to Andrea before anyone could answer, 'and I'll be on my way.'

'Of course.'

'No hard feelings, Jason?' Robert called after them just as they reached the hallway.

'Of course not, Robert,' snapped Jason without taking the trouble to turn around. 'As far as this family is concerned, I don't have any feelings at all.'

Andrea was silent as she led Jason up the staircase to the second floor. Perhaps Jason didn't deserve the same kind of inheritance as the brother who had stayed and worked for the company, but he deserved more than a box of books. He certainly didn't deserve the kind of callousness with which Creighton Dorning had so clinically discussed his childhood. Jason wasn't responsible for the conditions of his birth. That scandal belonged to Creighton Dorning and Roberta Carter, not to a child who had been innocent of all wrongdoing but who had paid the price by being an outsider all of his life.

When they reached the top of the long, curving stairway, Andrea turned right, glancing only briefly at the portraits that hung along the cream-coloured walls like ponderous reminders of the past. Creighton Dorning looked down, forbiddingly judgmental in a haze of dark brown oils, and further down the hall his wife Elizabeth smiled as she held a five-year-old Robert in her possessive arms. There was no portrait of the other Dorning son, and its very absence only served to echo the sentiments that had been expressed downstairs in the study. He might be Creighton's son, but he had never been a member of the Dorning family.

'I'm sorry your father said what he did,' she made an attempt to apologise for the injustices that had always followed Jason, 'that couldn't have been pleasant for you.'

'It wasn't.' Then, as if he were embarrassed by the simple truth, he changed the subject quickly.

'What are you up to these days, Andy? Or is going out with my brother enough for any woman?'

'I work.' She ignored the sarcasm in his voice. 'I'm an editor at Farraday Press now. Actually, I'm a junior editor. I'm the one who has to write rejection letters to all the heart-rendingly hopeful authors who send manuscripts.'

'Ah.' His smile was sympathetically good-natured, and quite attractive, Andrea noted with an unnerving sense of interest. 'It's hard to be rejected. I hope you have a gentle touch.'

'I try.' His eyes held hers so firmly she wondered for a moment whether he was talking about manuscripts or something else again. Then Jason glanced away, staring out of the window towards the chauffeur's cottage that was half-hidden beyond a copse of silvery-white birches.

'How did you get from there to here?' he asked her curiously. 'It's not usually a straight line, even for a pretty woman.'

'No . . .' She faltered momentarily, caught off guard by the casual way he'd delivered the compliment. 'After my father died, Creighton offered to pay my tuition and expenses to go to college. He called it "the Dorning Scholarship", but I knew it was a personal favour because he had liked my father.

'After that, one thing led to another,' Andrea shrugged. 'I wrote him letters telling him what I was studying and how I was getting along. I visited him from time to time, and he started to expect me on Thanksgiving and Christmas. Robert was busy most of the time, and I think Creighton was lonely. He told me once that he had fathered two sons, but he'd never had the pleasure of having children.'

'What kind of cancer killed him?' Jason interrupted, changing the subject once again.

'He had a growth in his intestine, but that's not . . .' She stopped herself before she said too much. Robert had put a great deal of effort into suppressing the cause of his father's death. All of that effort could be undone by telling Jason Dorning what had really happened.

'But what?' Jason asked suspiciously, noting her sudden uneasiness about the subject. 'Was there something else?'

'Officially, the cause of death was heart failure.'

'A heart attack, you mean?'

'Something like that,' she murmured evasively as she opened Creighton Dorning's bedroom door and followed Jason through it.

Nothing had changed since his father's death. A gilt-framed picture of Elizabeth still stood on his bedside. table, and the flannel bathrobe Andrea had given him for his birthday had been neatly folded at the foot of his carefully made bed. Even the decanter of his favourite brandy still remained on his dressing table. It was hard to believe that he was truly gone.

'Where did it happen?' Jason pressed for details. 'In his office, arguing about the price of kiwi fruit?'

'In bed.' She was irritated by his flippness. He might have been talking about someone he had never met, not the father who had tried, at least, to give his son an education and a place in the family business.

'Alone?'

'Yes!' snapped Andrea. 'Of course, alone!'

'Okay!' Jason held up his hands in a gesture of conciliation. 'I was just asking. My father was known to have an interest in women. I'm living proof of that.'

Andrea glared at him with undisguised distaste, and he met her stare without surprise, as if he expected the very anger he produced. ' "Welcome home, Jason," he said with sarcastic bitterness. "Just don't make the mistake of thinking that it's *your* home." Are you going to treat me like a leper, too, Andy?'

'I don't know what you mean.'

'Sure you do,' he snapped. 'There's some kind of little family secret here, and Robert has decided not to tell me what it is.'

There was a box on the window-seat on which Creighton had written the word 'Jason,' and Andrea turned to it now, opening the flap with a shaking hand to check the contents. 'This is the box of books your father wanted you to have,' she changed the subject abruptly. 'I'd like to keep the book he was reading when he died, if that's all right with you.'

'You can keep the whole damn box,' Jason muttered angrily, pulling out a cigarette and lighting it with a sharp thumbstroke against his silver lighter. 'That's not what I wanted from my father.'

What had he wanted? She sensed it was
something far more elusive than money or the
family business, some indication of acceptance and
belonging that had always been denied him. Even
now, by denying him the truth about his father's
death, Robert was keeping him outside the Dorning
family. And she was, too, she realised.

'He killed himself,' she blurted out before she lost
her courage. There was no change on his tense face,
no surprise or horror. He stared at her with dark,
still eyes as if he found her effort to tell him the truth
far more interesting than the truth itself.

'The pain must have been excruciating...'
Andrea groped for excuses to explain an act that she
considered wrong. 'I know he didn't want to be
bedridden and dependent, but Father Graham said
that...' She stopped herself, suddenly aware of
how ridiculous she must sound to a man like Jason.
He was too worldly to believe in the simple tenets of
a faith.

As if to reinforce her guess, his mouth twitched
upwards with cynical amusement. 'Are you afraid
my father's not tough enough for Hell, Andy? This
marriage he's arranged should be enough to prove
that theory wrong.'

'Don't laugh at me,' Andrea said defensively as
she glanced restlessly away from his derisive eyes. 'I
don't care what you think of my religion. And I
don't care what you think of your brother's
relationship with the chauffeur's daughter,' she
added firmly. 'I won't be ridiculed by ——'

'By the likes of me?' Jason suggested before she

had a chance to finish.

'By the likes of *anyone*,' she corrected coldly. 'Maybe your brother could do better, but he has chosen me.'

Jason stopped and stared at her a moment, as if he were considering her words. What happened next was too sudden and unexpected for Andrea to prevent. Jason caught her chin in his hand to lift it upward to the light. He studied her stunned eyes for a long moment, then his tense face relaxed into a smile. 'I didn't say he could do better, cupcake,' he suggested hoarsely as his hand fanned out against her back to hold her still. 'It's you who deserves a better deal.'

Her mistake was not pulling away at once when she still had a measure of a chance to break his hold around her. But she was too surprised to think of that until his mouth softened over hers and pressed down with firm insistence. It wasn't to be an affectionate, flirtatious kiss, she realised, filling with an irrational panic as his arms tightened to pull her close to the frighteningly masculine strength of his lean body.

Andrea pressed her palm against his shoulder, struggling feebly to push him back, but Jason didn't notice. His mouth widened once again and her defences fell before him like a sandcastle before a flooding sea. Her struggles stopped and she lay still against his chest, captive to the sensual promise in his warm embrace.

'Well . . .' Jason's gust of breath was a caress against her throat, and his delight was undisguised as he met her blue-grey eyes again with renewed curiosity. 'I enjoyed that, Andy. I wouldn't mind kissing you again.'

'I'm going to marry your brother,' she barely had the strength to answer. She closed her eyes to hide the tortured shame she felt at having so easily responded to the insistence of his arms. When she opened them again, the eyes she met were arrogantly amused.

Jason relaxed his hold and let her step away, although he followed her retreat with open interest. 'Lucky Robert,' he said in a voice that was laced with sarcastic cynicism. 'To inherit all that money and such a devoted woman, too!'

With those last words he shut the bedroom door behind him, leaving Andrea to stare at the polished wood with a mixture of exhilaration and uneasy fear.

CHAPTER TWO

ANDREA set aside the manuscript she had been reading and ran her hand across her forehead in a weary gesture. She had come back to face a heavy workload at the office, but that wasn't the reason she was so tired now. She hadn't slept well the night before, and now she was feeling the effects of her restless, anxious dreams.

There had been a compelling warmth in Jason's kiss, the kind of warmth she would have welcomed from the man she loved, and she was still unnerved by how easily she had responded to the firm direction of his arms. He was the one who had ended the embrace, she remembered now, wondering how long she would have lain still against him, surrendering to his will without a thought of stopping what she knew was thoroughly insane.

She hadn't stopped the kiss. Nor had she told Robert anything about it, partly because she didn't want to fan the flames of anger and resentment that already existed between the two Dorning men, and partly because she didn't want to explain her own mutinous reaction to Jason's mouth. It was only a kiss, she reasoned to herself, but no matter how she tried, she couldn't wipe the memory away with her usual common sense.

Nor could she wipe away the memories that had

flooded back all night. Jason Dorning at twenty had
been a romantically exotic man. Moody and
solitary, he had seemed like a restless cat who was
far too powerful for the confining cage of the
Dorning estate. But there had been another side to
him and he had shown it to the chauffeur's
daughter.

'*Jane Eyre*?' he had asked, stooping down to pick
up the book that had fallen from her arms. 'You
have to be careful with this kind of fiction, Andy.
It'll get inside your brain and make an incurable
romantic out of you.' He was teasing her, she
understood even then, although she never had a
ready answer and could only stare at him with such
breathless agitation she felt her pounding heart
would burst.

'Next you'll be reading *Wuthering Heights*, and
you'll spend the rest of your life looking for your
Heathcliff. Good little girls should stay away from
Heathcliffs,' Jason had admonished as he slid the
book underneath her arm.

The conversation would have been strange
enough if it had ended there, but Jason had called
out before she reached her door. 'I've got a copy of
it, in case you can't find it at the library.' His smile
was warm and generous when she turned to meet
his eyes. 'If you want to read it.'

He had lent her the book, then half a dozen
others, and before the summer was finished he was
showing her what he had written, too. It was all
wonderfully romantic prose, vibrantly written and
aching with a sensual yearning that inflamed her

senses. *He* inflamed her senses, Andrea remembered. Each glance was a caress, and every accidental touch had the power to jolt her like a shock, but Jason never knew that.

For him she was a diversion in a summer filled with increasing bitterness and argument, a naïve schoolgirl with whom he could play the role of gallant gentleman and teacher and from whom he could expect open admiration. For Jason there was an innocence about their friendship that Andrea had never felt.

Until the autumn day he said goodbye. 'You can keep the books I lent you,' he had said as she knelt down on the crackling, brown leaves that exuded a dry, bittersweet aroma around her. 'When I leave, I want to travel light.'

'Leave?' The word must have been a murmured question, but Andrea remembered it with a piercing clarity as if it reverberated through the crystal sharpness of the October air, spreadinq out in widening circles to fill the huge and frightening universe she suddenly saw without him.

Elizabeth didn't want him in the house, and the arguments with his father were growing worse each day. Creighton Dorning wanted his son to give up the ridiculous dream of being a writer and join the family business. 'Can you imagine me importing fruit for the rest of my life?' Jason had asked with a derisive smile, but Andrea couldn't give an answer. All that filled her mind was the aching echo of her grief.

'Andy?' Jason's fingers had softly touched her

shoulder and his other hand fanned out against her cheek, lifting her sad face into the waning evening light. Come with me, she willed his voice to say. I love you as much as you love me. 'Have you ever been kissed, little girl?' he asked instead as his thumb edged out to touch her trembling lower lip.

'Yes.'

'That's too bad,' he smiled. 'I wanted to be the first.' Then he leaned down to kiss her, letting his mouth soften over hers for only a brief moment before he let her go. 'Goodbye, Andy.' His voice hung in the violet shadows long after he stood up and strode away.

'Do you always work this late?'

The low, husky voice came from the doorway and Andrea looked up, so startled by the man who stood there that she could barely speak. She had been thinking about him, and he had appeared as if she had the power to conjure him from empty air. But that was ridiculous, she knew, shaking her head to dispel the fanciful direction of her thoughts. He had walked into the building like any other man, and his reason for coming here would be ordinary, too.

'I have to catch up on the work I didn't do the past two weeks,' she answered finally, glancing restlessly away from Jason's brown-eyed stare. Outside her office window the sky was the metallic lavender of a winter sunset, and the shadows in the hallway made Jason Dorning seem much larger and more powerful than he really was. 'Are you here to see someone?' she asked conversationally.

I've come to see you,' he answered as he stepped

into her office. 'I have something I want to talk to
you about, and I thought we could do it over
supper.'

'Supper?' she asked disapprovingly, conveying
her answer in her echo of his word. He had walked
out of her life ten years ago. She had waited for
letters that had never come, waited for the man she
loved to return to her, and finally given up the
waiting. Now that she planned to marry his brother
Robert, Jason was back with a dark-eyed moodi-
ness that raised an unwelcomed longing in her
dreams. Under the circumstances, she would have
to be insane to let him take her out to supper. 'I
don't think so, Mr Dorning. If you have something
to say to me, you can say it here.'

'Well...' He paused uncertainly. 'It's hard to
know where to begin.'

He was an ordinary man with an ordinary reason
for being here, Andrea reminded herself matter-of-
factly as she gathered up the manuscript that she'd
been reading. Jason's reason wasn't hard to guess.
He used to write. Quite well, as she remembered,
although she had adored him then and perhaps she
had seen his writing as more brilliant than it was.
She had expected a book by now, but in the past ten
years she'd seen nothing published under Jason
Dorning's name.

'Let me help you, then,' she offered evenly.
'You've got a novel that you want me to look at. It's
probably been rejected a dozen times, and now you
think the only way to get it published is to call in an
old favour. But you hate doing that,' she added

shrewdly, noting the way he paused and watched her as if he were calculating her reaction. 'The truth is that you're treading a very thin line between pride and desperation, and you certainly don't want to be laughed at by the chauffeur's skinny tomboy daughter.'

Jason didn't answer. He exhaled a breath and reached into his pocket for a cigarette, lighting it before it occurred to him to ask her if she minded. 'Can I smoke in here?' he asked, glancing around him for an ashtray. Andrea opened her desk drawer and took one out, which she set on the corner of her desk.

'I keep it for nervous authors.'

'All authors are nervous.'

'I suppose they are,' Andrea answered with a laugh. 'Would you sit down, Jason,' she suggested pointedly. 'If I have to watch you march back and forth in front of me in your sheepskin coat I'm going to fall asleep. And I don't think you want that.'

'No.' He eased himself down to the chair beside her desk and met her sympathetic eyes. 'You used to like my writing. But you were fifteen then,' he added, flicking a long, grey ash into the ashtray. 'And you were in love with me. Weren't you?'

'I suppose I was,' Andrea answered, deciding not to lie. 'That was just before I fell in love with Paul Newman.'

'And a long time before you fell in love with Robert,' he suggested evenly. 'If I had known how beautiful you were going to be when you grew up, I might have stayed around.'

He was lying, Andrea knew. He was so desperate to have someone in a publishing house look at his manuscript he was willing to say anything at all. 'You don't have to do this, Jason.'

'What?'

'Flatter me,' she answered. 'I'll read your book. Just don't lie to me, because that's an insult to my intelligence. And don't get your hopes up,' she went on before he had a chance to disagree. 'I can tell you what's wrong with the manuscript, and I can suggest ways to re-write it, but I can't buy it. The most I can do is recommend it to a senior editor.'

'That's fair enough.' He smiled so suddenly his face lifted upwards, setting laugh lines at the corners of his clear, brown eyes. Then he leaned forward to regard her with an impish look of mischief. 'What makes you think I need to re-write? Maybe I'm the next Jarvis Drew.'

'Good God, I hope not!' muttered Andrea, wrinkling up her nose.

Jason regarded her reaction with surprise. 'He's the best-selling author in the country!'

'Hm,' she muttered her agreement. 'Which just goes to show that sex and violence and bad writing sell very well in Peoria. Here in Boston we have higher standards.'

'You've read him?'

'Well . . . no,' she admitted reluctantly. 'Your father was a fan of his and he suggested that I read one of his books, but I couldn't get any farther than half a page. I've never liked detective stories.'

'Nice of you to give the man a chance before

condemning him.' Jason gave her a sarcastic smile that only served to irritate her. His criticism was right, of course. That made it so much worse.

'Well, it doesn't matter, does it?' she answered snappishly as she tossed her empty coffee cup into the waste paper basket. 'Jarvis Drew doesn't need me to approve or disapprove of his writing. Why don't you give me your manuscript and I'll read through it tonight.'

Jason opened his mouth as if he were going to pursue the subject, but he closed it again when she took her coat out of the cupboard and gathered up her bag. 'I'm going home now,' she announced, waiting beside the office door. 'Do you have the manuscript with you, Jason?'

'Hm?' he asked as if he had been startled out of his troubled thoughts. 'Oh, the manuscript . . . No, I . . . To tell the truth, it still needs a little work,' he admitted, following her out of the office and down the lighted hallway to the stairs. 'I think we should talk about it. Over supper,' he suggested firmly.

'No, I don't think so.' She cast him a wary sidelong glance, wondering now if he'd come to see her about his manuscript or if there was something else on Jason's mind. Of course there wasn't, she told herself pragmatically, dismissing her suspicions. His kiss had been nothing but a kiss. He had already forgotten it, and she would be wise to do the same.

'You copied Jarvis Drew's style, didn't you?' she guessed as she pushed open the front door and emerged into the frosty winter air. That was what was bothering him right now. Desperate for success, he had emulated the most successful writer in the country, and now he realised what she would say if she read his manuscript.

'He was a strong influence on my work,' Jason admitted, sliding his hands into his pockets as he matched her strides across the almost deserted car park toward her grey Toyota. 'I thought that's what editors were looking for.'

'You had a style of your own, Jason,' Andrea said kindly. 'It was wonderful, as I recall—romantic and honest. Go back and write the novel in your own style, and I'll take a look at it. I promise.'

'All right,' he agreed, leaning back against her car while she unlocked the door. Then he reached out to take the keys from her mittened hands. 'Let me drive,' he said decisively. 'I've already made reservations for supper.'

She had been crazy to let him take the keys, Andrea thought, following the maître d' to their table in the expensive Café Budapest. But Jason had been so insistent she had given in.

'I shouldn't be here with you,' she admitted as she cast a frankly concerned glance at the prices on the elegantly printed page. If he was trying to impress her by bringing her to one of the most expensive restaurants in Boston, he was being entirely too reckless with his money.

'You don't like Hungarian food?'

'I'm going to marry your brother,' she reminded him. 'What do you think he's going to say when he finds out I came here with you?'

'Who's going to tell him?' Jason asked her. 'You don't run to him and blurt out every little indiscretion, do you?'

'No.' She felt a little foolish under his questioning stare. Then she realised what she was saying. 'There haven't been any indiscretions,' she corrected evenly, wondering why she found Jason's slow, assessing smile so attractive when it should have irritated her instead. 'And there won't be! This isn't!' she insisted firmly. 'We're going to discuss your book. It's a business supper.' What she had meant to sound firm and businesslike came out in a wavering tone as if it had been a question.

His smile spread even wider before he returned his attention to the menu. 'Relax, angel,' he said reassuringly. 'I won't seduce you before dessert.'

'Where was I?' Jason asked, refilling Andrea's wine glass before she had a chance to object.

'You had just left England and you were completely broke.' She gave him a warm smile, encouraging him to continue talking about his travels. The wine had relaxed her wary suspicion of Jason's motives, but it was more than that. It wasn't difficult to listen to Jason Dorning's stories. He had woven wonderful tales of exotic places she had always longed to see, and he had filled those stories with eccentric details that made his wanderings come alive.

'I have a friend who raises horses in the Camargue,' Jason continued, his low, masculine voice vibrating with pleasure at the memories. 'I worked for him long enough to get some money. I was there for the annual pilgrimage of the gypsies. You would have enjoyed that, Andy.'

'Were there really gypsies?' she asked with open interest.

'Mm-hm. Fifteen thousand of them gather in the town of Les Saintes Maries for the blessing of their patron saint, Sara the Egyptian. They're wonderful horse traders. And honest in their own way. The people of the Camargue say that a gypsy never steals more than he can use, which is something they don't say about their government officials.'

'And after that?' she asked him eagerly, barely noticing that they had finished supper and that the waiter hovered, waiting to remove their plates.

'I went on to Brazil.'

'Why Brazil?'

'Because it was there and I wasn't. Do you want coffee?' Jason asked, pulling out a cigarette and lighting it with a sharp thumbflick against his silver lighter. 'Or a liqueur?'

'Both. I'll have a Grand Marnier.'

'The lady wants it all,' he teased her in a deliberately seductive voice. 'I like that in a woman.' His lips tipped upward into an easy smile, but he didn't wait for Andrea to give an answer. He turned to the waiter instead. 'Two coffees and a Grand Marnier,' he ordered.

Andrea's fingers touched the silver lighter he had left in the middle of the table and she turned it over to read the engraved inscription. 'To Jason, from your *bien-aimée*.' He had left out the most interesting part of his adventures, Andrea guessed, replacing the lighter on the table. She didn't doubt that Jason had known his share of women. He was an attractive man.

'Tell me, Andy,' he said slowly, noting the hand that lingered on his lighter, 'who suggested that you date my brother? Robert? Or my father?'

'Robert.' She stiffened imperceptibly. She had always suspected that it had been Creighton Dorning's suggestion that Robert ask her out. Creighton had certainly made no secret of his feelings. He had wanted Robert to marry Andrea McKinley. 'Why?' she asked suspiciously. 'Don't you think I'm Robert's type?'

It might have been easier if Jason had snapped a sarcastic answer, but he didn't say a word. He simply looked at her with eyes so fathomlessly dark that she could barely breathe. 'He isn't a snob about my being the chauffeur's daughter,' she went on as best she could.

'I see.' His voice was far too even, Andrea thought, casting him a quick glance to note the harshness of his face. 'So, Robert doesn't mind that you're the chauffeur's daughter, and you don't mind that he's a millionaire?'

'That's not why I'm marrying him.'

'What else is there?'

'He's very attractive,' she explained, running her finger distractedly along the table to trace the barely discernible white pattern on the white background of the tablecloth. 'He's bright and well-read, and he's an interesting conversationalist. We share a common interest in classical music and good art . . .'

'I wonder . . .' said Jason as he leaned forward to balance his chin against his hands, '. . . if you're going to tell me that you love him.'

'I do.' She met his eyes then, forcing herself to hold his stare despite the fluttering that gripped her stomach. She had thought that she loved Robert Dorning until Jason had sauntered back into her life, and now, for the first time, she felt misgivings.

A little doubt was normal, she reasoned with herself. All she had was wedding jitters, but she sensed that her neatly ordered world would fall apart if she let Jason see that weakness. 'I'm going to marry him, Jason,' she said firmly. 'We love each other very much, and I'm going to marry him, just like your father wanted.'

'I see.' His voice was far more threatening than the smile that edged up at the corners of his mouth, but even that was far too cold and wilful for Andrea's peace of mind. He might have pursued the subject if the waiter hadn't interrupted to set their coffee cups in front of them. Jason drank his coffee silently, but when she glanced up she met his stubborn eyes.

'You were going to tell me about your book,' she suggested, searching for a topic that would turn the conversation away from her relationship with Robert. 'Is it about your travels?'

'It's about you.' His eyes met hers so earnestly that she glanced away with evasive fear. Why was

this man capable of moving her to a hundred
emotions she didn't want to feel? She was engaged
to marry someone else, and only an idiot would
throw that away because she had a restless longing
for a dark-eyed man who had stepped out of her
past.

'I'm afraid you've chosen a very dull topic.'

'Not at all, Andy. People have always been
fascinated by witches.'

'What?'

'You don't have to pretend innocence,' he
answered evenly, leaning back to take a sip of
coffee. 'I know you're a witch, and you know I know
it. I spent enough time being tortured by your
spells.' Andrea was silent, bewildered by the
insanity of his accusation. 'One minute my tongue
was made of lead, and the next minute my heart
pounded until I was afraid it would explode. I was
consumed by flames more than once,' he added
with a smile that ached with pent-up mischief. 'I
think you must have been perfecting your "setting
hungry men on fire" spell that summer.'

The man was making fun of her, Andrea realised,
flushing with irritation. She had been a perfectly
ordinary girl who had grown up into a perfectly
plain woman. She wasn't going to have her head
turned by crazy compliments that made no earthly
sense.

'I had to run away before I was completely
incinerated,' Jason continued matter-of-factly,
lighting a cigarette and watching the white smoke
coil sinuously above his head. 'I ran for my life,' he

echoed. 'But I always knew I'd come back eventually, and when I did, I'd have to have some magic of my own.'

'And do you?' Andrea asked bluntly, glancing restlessly away when his amused eyes met her stare. Jason Dorning was being fanciful, but he wasn't being subtle. 'I'll bet you do,' she murmured, unimpressed. 'I'll bet you've studied everywhere you could.'

'I'm not a virgin,' Jason shrugged. Then his mouth edged upward into a smile. 'Are you?'

'That's none of your business,' she retorted sharply, so furious at his lack of manners she dared to meet his stare at last. 'Only a philistine would ask.'

Even that amused him. 'There you are, Andy,' he said so appreciatively she couldn't keep her defiant frostiness for long. 'Freeze me into a block of ice with those violet eyes of yours. Prove that the witch is still alive.'

'My eyes are blue.'

'Not when you're angry,' he disagreed. 'When you're angry, you're a violet-eyed gypsy queen.'

'I'm a gypsy now?' she demanded disapprovingly, wondering if he thought she was still a lovestruck fifteen-year-old who hung on his every teasing word. 'Do you think I believe any of this flattery?'

'I think you'd like to.'

Andrea fell silent, knowing that anything she said would be twisted around another way by Jason Dorning's sharp-tongued ridicule.

'There's something I don't understand,' he

continued in a relentlessly soft voice that tore at her jumpy nerves. 'Why has the witch disguised herself as a serving girl? "Yes, Robert . . . No, Robert. I'll get it for you right away, Robert," ' He imitated her patient helpfulness with a sure-centred cruelty. 'Why doesn't your magic work on him, Andy? Why can't you freeze *him* into a block of ice with your violet eyes? Maybe he doesn't love you enough.' He answered his own question.

'You're being cruel, Jason,' she objected. 'And I don't find it enjoyable. I'm going home,' she announced, reaching for her bag, but Jason seized her wrist to stop her.

'Don't leave before you hear me out. I didn't bring you here to hurt you.'

'Then why *did* you bring me here?' she demanded.

'Because a long time ago I knew a little girl who liked me when no one else did,' Jason answered evenly, softening his hold against her wrist, although he didn't let her go completely. 'I used to know what you wanted out of life, Andy. You wanted a man who was capable of setting the stars on fire when he touched you. Didn't you?'

Andrea didn't answer. She had wanted him, but he had left her without a backward glance. She wasn't going to make the mistake of loving a man like him again, she told herself firmly, although she could feel that resolve crumbling as his thumb softly stroked her hand, reminding her of all the touches she had once longed for from Creighton Dorning's moody younger son.

'I was fifteen then,' she reminded him. 'And my head was filled with romantic nonsense. I've grown up since then.'

'Have you, love?' He smiled as if he doubted what she said. 'Or have you learned that there's a difference between what you want and what a man can give? Some men,' he corrected. 'Some men can give more than others, and I think you know that.'

'Some men have more arrogance than others,' she snapped tartly, trying to dispel the tangled web of sensuality he was deliberately weaving around her aching senses. 'I'm not fifteen any more, and I have no intention of standing in line to become another *bien-aimée* to an impoverished, unpublished writer. In case that's what you're offering.'

Jason's jaw tightened with impatience and his hand slipped away from hers. Say no, she silently implored him. Tell me that you've come back because you've always loved me.

'You've got tough, Andy,' he admitted with a smile of grudging admiration. 'All right. I brought you here to propose a partnership. It offends my sense of romance to see a woman like you settle for less than you could have. If you love my brother enough to marry him, the least I can do is bring him to his knees for you. Consider it a wedding present.'

'Oh.' She was disappointed. For one short moment she had wondered if he was suggesting that he marry her himself, but that wasn't what Jason had in mind. He wanted to make Robert jealous. 'What would you get out of this?' she asked suspiciously. 'Other than the obvious pleasure of torturing your brother?'

'Part of the estate,' Jason answered without hesitation. 'I think Robert would be willing to make a deal if he were worried about competition.'

'I see,' Andrea said coolly. He expected Robert to pay him to go away, and she suspected Robert might do just that if she were willing to go along with this crazy plan. But she wasn't. She wasn't the type of woman who played games, especially ones as dangerous as this. She was already far too attracted to Jason Dorning, and far too angry that his suggestive, romantic conversation had led to this.

And she was disappointed in him, she admitted to herself. This was the man she had idolised ten years ago. Now, seeing him with adult eyes, she realised that he was nothing but a con man and a swindler.

'I don't think so, Jason,' she said, picking up her bag. 'I'm not interested in making my fiancé jealous. Send me your manuscript when you get it re-written. If it's as inventive as your plot to get part of the inheritance, it might have a chance.'

CHAPTER THREE

'I WANTED to come here tonight to see how Rombauld presents the vegetables,' Robert admitted as the waiter placed two bright blue plates in front of them. A collection of doll-sized carrots and beets fanned out at the top of Andrea's plate, and at the bottom, below a tiny serving of creamed lobster, there were two minuscule courgettes still adorned with withered blossoms, and a tiny ear of corn. The food was absolutely beautiful, a work of art, if nothing else, but there wasn't very much of the exquisite product.

'My father was far too conservative with the company,' Robert said as he set his napkin in his lap. 'This is the coming trend—miniature vegetables, the new gourmet products like fiddlehead ferns and radicchio, the loquats and atemoyas that people are developing a taste for in the tropics. We could create a whole new market, Andrea,' he said enthusiastically. 'We could be the biggest importers of gourmet produce in the country if we could sign the growers to exclusive contracts.'

Andrea didn't make an answer, nor did Robert need one. It hadn't been that way with Jason. He had weighed each word she said, and he had watched her closely to sense the words that she kept private. It was all for one purpose, she reminded

herself as she speared a tiny carrot. His attention
might be flattering, but his motives certainly were
not.

What he was proposing was a form of blackmail,
and while she thought he deserved more of the
inheritance than he had been given, she didn't
admire the way Jason planned to go about getting
what he considered his rightful share. She was going
to marry Robert, and she wasn't going to play
games with another man—certainly not with a man
who could move her to a hundred different
emotions in the course of one evening's meal.

'I've made a reservation at the Hermitage Hotel
in Virginia for the Christmas holidays,' Robert
announced, cutting into his medallion of beef
tenderloin. 'While we're there we can visit Judge
Sanderson. He's an old family friend who'd be
delighted to marry us. I hope that meets with your
approval.'

'Yes,' Andrea agreed as she sipped her wine. 'A
Christmas wedding sounds wonderfully romantic.'

'It will work out nicely on several accounts. No
one can criticise us for being ostentatious so soon
after Father's death. And the Harmons are going to
be at the Hermitage. I can conduct business while
we're there.'

'Oh.' Andrea tried to keep the disappointment
out of her voice. They were flying to Virginia to be
married. Just this once she wished that Robert
would think of nothing else. And she wished that he
had proposed a little more romantically. 'We'll get
married, then,' wasn't exactly her idea of high

romance, or low romance, or anything in between.

Jason Dorning wouldn't have put it so coldly, Andrea thought, remembering the insistence of his mouth as he bent down to kiss her. He was arrogant and greedy, but he wouldn't have assumed he knew her feelings quite as easily as Robert had. She pushed a piece of lobster around her plate with distracted irritation, wondering why something that she had wanted was suddenly so uninteresting now that it was hers.

'Andrea?'

She looked up, realising that it wasn't the first time that Robert had said her name. 'I asked you if anything is on your mind? You haven't heard a word I've said.'

'I'm sorry, Robert.' She put down her fork and focused her attention on his face. Jason's plot was already working, undermining the patient interest she had always taken in Robert's conversations. 'I've been distracted. Something very odd happened yesterday.'

'At work?'

'No. It was something else. Something personal and . . .' Andrea sat up a little straighter, staring past Robert's shoulder to the foyer of the restaurant. Was it her imagination, or was Jason Dorning there?

It wasn't Jason, she decided, returning her attention to Robert's face. She was imagining things. But a moment later the same man stepped into the dining room and made his way between the tables, closer and closer to the table where they sat.

'Robert!' Jason clapped his brother on the shoulder with a heartiness that was patently pretended. Then, before Robert could object, he pulled up a chair and joined them at the table.

'I hope I'm not interrupting a *moment intime*.' He didn't wait for an answer before he cast a broad, friendly smile in Andrea's direction. 'How are you tonight, cupcake?'

'Fine,' she answered, too surprised to object to his overt flippancy.

'How did you know we were here?' Robert demanded, unimpressed by Jason's jovial good spirits.

'I called your office and said I was your brother,' Jason admitted. 'It's amazing how well honesty can work. I should use it more often.' Andrea recognised the statement as a joke, but Robert missed the humour. 'At any rate, I was thinking about what happened at the house the other day, and I've decided to tender an apology. You are my brother, and I owe you more civility than I showed.'

'Oh!' Robert was taken completely by surprise. 'Very well, then,' he said graciously, holding out his hand. 'I accept your apology. I wasn't very civil myself.'

'I should apologise to Andy, too,' Jason admitted as he shook his brother's hand. 'Can you forgive me for kissing you, love?'

So that was why he was here, Andrea thought, noting Jason's infuriating smile of mock concern, and then Robert's balefully angry eyes. Jason had decided to cause trouble whether or not she agreed to his ludicrous plot to make Robert jealous.

'What kiss?' Robert demanded coldly.

'Jason was congratulating me on our engagement,' Andrea tried to reassure him, but Jason's
eyes were far too impishly amused for her to think
he meant to let it pass as a brotherly gesture of
congratulations. 'I didn't even remember it until
this moment. It was really nothing.'

'You call that kiss *nothing*, cupcake?' Jason
pretended to be hurt.

'Less than nothing,' she corrected evenly.

'Andrea is *not* your cupcake,' Robert interrupted
peevishly, pushing his plate aside. 'I'd like to know
what you thought you were doing, kissing my
fiancée like that.'

'I made a pass at Andy for the pure pleasure of
kissing a beautiful woman. And I'll probably do it
again if I get the chance.'

Jason's voice was as caressing as his eyes, a
warm, sweet tone that flowed across her senses,
raising a desire that excited her so strangely she had
to look away. It was a game to infuriate Robert, she
reminded herself practically, but she couldn't
ignore the unnerving sense of pleasure she felt at
Jason's words.

Robert glared at Jason. 'I think it would be best if
you stayed away from . . .'

'Excuse me,' the waiter interrupted. 'Would you
like to order, sir?'

'Jason is leaving,' Robert answered bluntly.

'Am I?' he asked innocently, fixing Robert with

amused, dark eyes. 'I don't have other plans. I can stay all night.'

'Then *we're* leaving,' Robert decided, dropping his napkin on the table. 'May we have the check, please?'

Even their hasty departure did nothing to dissuade Jason Dorning. He followed them out of the restaurant and along the street. 'I walked through the Commons on the way over here,' Jason volunteered conversationally as he fell into step beside Andrea. 'I'd forgotten how pretty it is this time of year with all the Christmas lights. Do you remember the time you were babysitting for the two Richardson girls and we brought them into the city to see the lights?'

'*I* brought them into the city,' Andrea corrected. 'We ran into you by coincidence.'

'Are you sure it was coincidence?' Jason asked her teasingly. 'There were a lot of coincidental meetings that year. At the pool, in the woods, on your way home from school. I always seemed to be running into you somewhere.'

It was true, Andrea realised, giving him a curious, sidelong glance. Long before she had developed her schoolgirl crush on him, she had run into him by accident in half a dozen places. It had never occurred to her that those meetings were anything but accidental.

'Anyway,' he went on before she could give an answer, 'you told the girls a story about the lights. Do you remember what it was?'

'No.'

'You said that they were fairy trees,' he volunteered. 'You said that every light was a fairy holding a lover's heart, and after Christmas they all flew off to hide among the stars. Far away into the stars,' his voice continued, so low and seductive she was caught up in the spell of the old memories that he was weaving deliberately around her. 'If a lover wanted to reclaim his heart, his only chance was to go to the Commons on Christmas Eve and snatch it from the trees. And if he missed that chance, he'd be condemned to think of his love for ever after, whenever he gazed up at the sky.'

Yes, Andrea thought. She remembered that romantic story and how much the Richardson twins had loved it. She had to tell it to them at bedtime for months after that excursion to see the Christmas lights. 'That's *my* heart up there.' Jason had told the girls, pointing to a glimmering light at the very pinnacle of the tallest maple. 'I don't suppose I'll ever get it back.'

'That was your story,' she reminded him. 'You told the twins it was your Christmas present to them.' Jason shoved his hands inside his pockets to keep them warm in the chilling December cold, but his face was a warm glow as if he were touchingly pleased that she remembered. 'I wrote it down in my diary because I thought you were going to be a famous writer someday.'

'I remember that diary,' he agreed. 'It had a battered blue cover and you treated it like the single greatest treasure on this earth.'

'Yes,' Andrea smiled, 'I suppose I did.'

'And one day I found you asleep under the oak in the yard, clutching that book tightly to your chest,' he went on as he loped along beside her in the frosty air. 'I knew you had written about me, but I was too much of a gentleman to read it.'

'You couldn't have got it away from me without waking me up,' Andrea retorted with a laugh. 'Don't make yourself out to be more of a gentleman than you really were.'

Robert stalked along beside them in sullen silence, visibly relieved when they reached a pale blue Mercedes parked along the kerb. 'We can't drop you anywhere,' he muttered, leaning down to slide the key into the door. 'We're going in the opposite direction.'

'You always were,' Jason snapped back drily, waiting until Robert's back was turned before he slid his arm through Andrea's. 'Do you know that you have something on the corner of your mouth?' He changed the subject suddenly, using his finger to lift her face into the street lamp's glow. It was an ancient trick, but Jason moved so quickly she didn't know his kiss was coming until his mouth met hers.

Her mouth softened automatically under the command of his until she had granted a possession that surprised her. 'Hey!' cried Robert, infuriated. Just as suddenly as the kiss had come, it ended. Jason let her go and stepped away, eluding Robert's grasp with a quick laugh of triumph.

'I'm warning you, Jason!'

'That's fair enough,' Jason goaded, backing towards the corner. 'Consider my kiss a warning, too. Sweet dreams, cupcake!' He raised his hand to wave and she automatically waved back, unexpectedly giddy from the excitement of his kiss.

The kiss had been as much an act as everything else that Jason had done that evening, but no matter how she tried she couldn't keep a smile from twitching upward at the corners of her mouth. Robert noted that with undisguised dismay. 'You can't have enjoyed that?' he demanded as he turned the key to start the engine. 'No woman wants a man who simply takes what he wants.'

'No ... Of course not,' Andrea murmured, pulling her lips down into a neutral line as she smoothed her coat across her knees. No woman in her right mind would want the attentions of a flamboyant pirate like Jason Dorning when she could have the steady, rational affection of a man like Robert. No woman in her right mind would *believe* a man like Jason, but his romantic stories touched a part of her that she had forgotten she possessed—that hidden part of her that longed to believe in the miracle of love.

Jason's attentions had more to do with money than with love, she reminded herself bluntly. But her mouth still burned with a strange excitement, as if his kiss had branded her with a mark of the thief's possession, and she found herself straining for a sight of him as they rounded the corner on to Tremont Street.

'Jason doesn't want me,' Andrea admitted honestly as she made a pot of coffee in her kitchen. 'I'm not exactly his type.'

'You walk and you breathe,' Robert answered cynically. 'Jason doesn't seem to ask much more from women.'

'He wants you to pay him to go away,' Andrea said as she took the milk from the refrigerator and filled a small ceramic pitcher. 'He thinks he deserves part of the inheritance, and maybe he does. He *is* your brother. But that's not the issue anyway,' she continued when Robert opened his mouth to object. 'The issue between us is trust. I'm not a mindless idiot, Robert. I didn't fall for his flattery last night, and I'm not going to fall for . . .' She stopped herself with a groan. She *was* a mindless idiot.

'Last night?' Robert came around the counter with peevishly dark eyes. 'What happened last night?'

'Nothing. We had supper together to discuss a manuscript he wants me to read. And that was that.' She shrugged with what she hoped would look like casual disinterest.

'Where did he take you for supper?'

'Nowhere. Some little place that serves Hungarian food.'

'What little place exactly?' Robert pressed the question, much to Andrea's exasperation. Why didn't he take the situation at face value and leave the rest alone?

'The Café Budapest,' she muttered, turning away to unplug the coffee pot and place it on a lacquered tray. 'Do you want to know what we ordered?'

'I want to know where he gets that kind of money.'

'I don't know!' Andrea snapped, out of patience with his sullen inquisition. 'I don't believe this.' She pressed a cooling palm against her face and took a breath to calm her sudden anger. 'This is what he wants, Robert. Can't you see what he's doing?'

'I can see clearly enough,' muttered Robert. 'I could see how flattered you were when he kissed you.'

'Because—women are flattered by attention.' She attempted a reasonable, calm voice. 'Even when we know it's all a pack of lies. It's—I don't know, Robert. Maybe it's a genetic flaw in females. We like hearing that we're beautiful, even when we're not.'

'I should think you'd have more sense.'

For some reason that comment hit a nerve straight-on and Andrea stiffened with irritation, but she forced herself to let her anger pass. This was Jason's fault. He had introduced doubt and jealousy into a rational, affectionate relationship. She shouldn't take her anger out on Robert when Jason was to blame.

'I have plenty of common sense,' she disagreed, balancing the tray against her hip to carry it to the living room where she placed it on the coffee table. 'I know that the best way to handle Jason is to humour him and go on about my business. He likes to cause an uproar, and if we don't give him one he'll get bored and go away.' She eased herself down to the couch and poured them each a cup of fragrantly steaming coffee.

Robert joined her there, considering her words with a thoughtful, strained expression. 'I suppose you're right,' he conceded finally, lacing his fingers through hers as he met her eyes with an appreciatively warm smile. 'You are a very level-headed, intelligent . . .'

He got no further with the compliment before the phone rang with an insistent shrill. 'Hello?' said Andrea as she picked it up and held it to her ear.

'Hi.' The greeting was innocent enough, but the tone was something altogether different. It was soft and silken like a touch and left no doubt as to the identity of the late-night caller.

'Hello, Jason,' Andrea said evenly, glancing up to cast a reassuring smile in Robert's direction. 'Have you called to talk to your brother?'

'Is *he* still there?' The voice was peevish now. 'Does he think he's going to . . .' Jason hesitated as if the thought were new. 'Is he going to stay the night?' he demanded bluntly. 'You don't let him take advantage of you like that, do you?'

'No, of course he isn't!' She snapped an answer before she realised the idiocy of her defensiveness. Why did she have to explain anything to Jason? *Robert* was the man she meant to marry.

'Well, that's good,' said Jason, relieved. 'I know you're a big girl, cupcake. And, lord knows, I don't expect a woman to be a nun in this day and age, but I think life would be easier all around if you didn't jump in the sack with Robert. Do you know what I'm saying?'

Andrea stared at the phone incredulously.

'Sex is a powerful force, Andy,' he reminded her in the tone of a strict but kindly uncle talking to a dim-witted little girl. 'Especially for you. You're the romantic type. You always have been. I think you could get carried away and do things for all the wrong reasons, and if I'm not there to protect you . . .' He stopped abruptly when Andrea burst into a stifled giggle.

'Oh, damn!' he muttered. 'Okay, I know I'm being an idiot,' he admitted tersely. 'I just can't help worrying about you. I know I'm stirring up a lot of feelings . . . and I think . . . Look,' he tried again, faltering painfully for words, 'promise me you won't do anything stupid.'

'I won't.'

'Wait until you're sure about your feelings. Promise me that, Andy.'

There was so much desperation in his voice that she wondered if this really was an act. If it wasn't, his concern for her was very sweet and touching. 'I promise, Jason. I'm sorry I laughed at you.'

She heard his sigh of relief, but she didn't hear the words that followed. Robert took the receiver from her hands and firmly hung it up. 'I don't want you to talk to him again,' he said firmly.

Jason wasn't doing anything wrong, she thought, annoyed with Robert for the imperiousness of his demand. Why should she live in an ivory tower simply because Robert didn't trust his brother? Or her either, she thought angrily. Wasn't that what he was saying?

'Andrea?' Robert's voice was edged with fear. She met his eyes, surprised for one brief moment that he was still beside her. Then she roused herself from thought and studied his tense face. He wasn't a cold tyrant, dictating the terms of their relationship. He had cared about her long before he knew the terms of his father's will. 'I'm sorry,' he admitted quietly. 'I shouldn't have taken the phone away from you, but I don't want you to get hurt.'

He was probably right, Andrea knew. Jason had a way of knocking her off guard and side-stepping her defences until she was dizzy with confusion. Her common sense screamed out for her to cling to Robert, but she was learning, much to her dismay, that there was something stronger than dreary common sense.

'Let's sit down and finish our coffee,' he suggested. 'Perhaps we should talk about Jason and what he's doing to us.'

'I'm very tired, Robert,' answered Andrea evenly. The last thing in the world she wanted to discuss with Robert was Jason Dorning and the effect he had on her. Everything he said was lies, but when he met her eyes with his dark-eyed, hungry stare she knew that she was capable of believing all the lies he told. 'I'd like to go to bed now, if you don't mind.'

'All right,' Robert agreed reluctantly, picking up his coat as Andrea opened her apartment door. He stopped in front of her and studied her pale face as if he were seeing her for the first time. Then he leaned down and kissed her. Not distractedly. Not with his usual affectionate gentleness. This time his arms curved around her with more power than she'd suspected he possessed, and his mouth met hers with the full intensity of a lover's hunger.

She was so surprised she barely moved at first, and then her arms came up to hold him, giving him encouragement as he deepened his caress. But no matter how she willed it, she couldn't keep herself from imagining that it was another man who held her, a man who could set the stars on fire with his touch.

CHAPTER FOUR

GOOD old Andrea McKinley, she thought self-mockingly as she stood on the granite stoop of her apartment building. She was too bright to fall for Jason's empty flattery, too reasonable to mistake a physical desire for anything more satisfying. Why then did she feel suddenly dissatisfied with everything in her calm and ordered life?

She had responded to Robert's kiss, giving him a full measure of the sensual reassurance he was asking, but it was Jason's mouth that lingered in her dreams. It was Jason's eyes that seemed to see her aching longing for an excitement she couldn't name, and it was Jason's voice, so low and masculine, that wove idiotically romantic fairy tales through her weary mind.

Forget him, she thought sternly, shoving her gloved hands into the pockets of her camel coat. She was engaged to an attractive, wealthy man, and Jason Dorning could promise nothing except a brief desire and an awful lot of trouble Andrea McKinley didn't need.

Still, he had reminded her that there was a place for change and excitement in the world. With that thought in mind she had made an appointment with a hairdresser for later in the afternoon. For Robert, she told herself without conviction. Robert was the

57

man she loved, and the man that she should please.

'She stood against the flooding moonlight, her alabaster cheeks demanding the worship of my kiss.'

The words were strange enough, but the voice that delivered them sent an electric thrill through her jangled nerves. Andrea turned just enough to see the man who leaned his chin against the railing, regarding her with a musing half-smile of appreciation.

'I'm not standing in the moonlight.' She forced her voice to calmness as she answered Jason's effusively poetic greeting. 'And you can keep your kiss. I've had quite enough of those already.'

Why, in God's name, was she so happy to see him? Andrea wondered, ashamed of her own mutinously irrational reactions to the man. He could only cause her trouble, but when she looked at him she knew that she was inviting all the trouble he could give.

'You've been standing on this stoop for five minutes. I was afraid you'd been turned to stone by one of your own spells.'

'No.' He wasn't far from the truth, she knew, making a show of opening her bag and searching through it for her shopping list. 'I was thinking of what I need to buy today. Christmas is two and a half weeks away, and I'm woefully unprepared this year. Your father's death and then the wedding plans ——' She stopped, flushed with irritation as Jason's mouth curved upward into a sarcastic smile.

'Hm,' he murmured his agreement. 'Two tragedies in one season does seem a bit unfair.' Then, before she could give an answer, he joined her on the stairs. 'Let's go and buy you some new clothes. I'll bet you have a decent body underneath that rummage sale layered look you affect.'

'I'll bet you have some manners underneath your arrogance!' Andrea snapped, fixing him with a furiously stern stare. 'My clothes aren't any of your business, and neither is my body.'

'I'm a writer,' he reminded her, following her down the steps to the pavement and then across the street. 'Everything that interests me is my business.'

'Cute,' she snapped sarcastically.

'Thank you. I think you're nice, too.' Then a moment later his amused voice called out again. 'Especially your backside. You move it very nicely.'

Andrea stopped short and turned around, waiting until Jason strolled up beside her. 'Read my lips, Jason,' she said firmly. 'I am engaged to your brother. You can't follow me around the city making personal remarks about my body.'

'You don't want me to follow you around talking about fruit and vegetables, do you? That would be a bore.'

'No.' Andrea took a breath to calm her impatience with Jason's feigned innocence. 'I don't think you should follow me around at all. Robert wouldn't like it.'

'Ah!' He shoved his hands into his pockets and gave her a boyish grin. 'Now *there's* a reason. How is the overgrown Eagle Scout these days? Jealous?

Cranky? Tyrannical?' he asked with far too much relish. 'Or is he the type who gets whiney and insecure?'

'No, as a matter of fact.' Andrea decided to fight Jason's fire with a little of her own. 'He gets romantic. You've done me a big favour, Jason.'

'Oh.' Jason wasn't pleased. It was strange how much he looked like Robert at that moment, she thought, wondering why she was so pleased at Jason's irritation. Perhaps because there was poetic justice in the situation. He had been so arrogantly sure of his own attractiveness he hadn't expected his brother to do anything but pay him to leave town. He certainly hadn't expected Robert to rise to the competition. And neither had she, she realised, delighted by the possibilities.

'Goodbye, Jason.' She strode off along the street, smiling when she heard the sound of footsteps behind her. It probably wasn't to her credit, she thought, but she was beginning to enjoy being chased.

'What are we going to do today?' Jason changed the subject suddenly as he slipped his arm through hers to stop her striding progress down the street.

'I've got an appointment at two-thirty.'

'With whom?'

'Maybe it's with a psychiatrist,' Andrea retorted, wondering why she didn't object more strongly to his outrageous arrogance or to the arm that casually circled her waist to coax her along the shop-lined street.

'You don't need a psychiatrist.' Jason dismissed

the suggestion with a brief, impatient gesture. 'You're no crazier than I am.'

Andrea's only answer was a laugh.

Andrea followed Jason's gaze through the glass in Jordan Marsh's window, waiting for the toy train that would emerge any minute from a plastic tunnel, bearing Santa Claus and a full load of gifts. She hadn't shopped for Robert's Christmas present as she had planned. Instead, she and Jason had walked in a leisurely manner around the city, looking at the displays in all the windows.

'Your appointment's at a tattoo parlour, isn't it?' he teased, leaning against the building to study her pink, wind-chilled cheeks. 'Would you like a tattoo?'

'I wouldn't do anything that permanent.'

'Certainly not,' he baited her. 'Getting a tattoo would be as stupid as marrying one man when you're attracted to another. I've got an idea, Andy,' he suggested before she had a chance to answer. 'Why don't you sleep with me and get me out of your system?'

Was that his idea of a joke? Andrea wondered irritably. Even if she were the type to spend the night with a man so casually she doubted that would be a sure-fire way to get Jason out of her restless dreams. 'Is that what usually happens?' she retorted evenly. 'Once a woman sleeps with you she knows there's nothing to come back for?'

'Nice one,' grinned Jason, not at all offended by the insult. 'You're getting better at this, cupcake.

Okay,' he admitted, slipping his arm through hers again, 'why don't you sleep with me and let me get you out of *my* system? Call it charity. I need to get on with my life.'

'Aren't you too proud to take charity?'

'Nope.'

'Maybe you'd fall in love with me,' she suggested, trying to keep her voice as teasingly flirtatious as his had been. She was already half in love with him, although she chose to treat the emotion as a temporary aberration, Something akin to a touch of 'flu that would clear up with time and the proper medicine. 'What would happen to your plans then?'

'I suppose I'd have to marry you,' he answered with a shrug. 'It wouldn't be such a bad life. I'd get someone to edit my manuscripts and wash my socks. You could carry my luggage . . .' His mouth tipped upward just enough to tell her he was teasing. Jason Dorning couldn't even take marriage seriously. 'You could bring me my newspaper and my slippers at the end of a long day . . .'

'Great,' Andrea responded with a laugh. 'What would I get out of this arrangement?'

'Other than me?' He asked the question as if no more was needed to make any woman's life complete, but he grew serious when she fixed him with a cool, sarcastic stare. 'I can give you things, Andy,' he said evenly. 'Maybe I don't have as much money as Robert, but I can show you places you've never seen. Introduce you to people. I've got friends who are a damn sight more interesting than fruit importers.'

'Name one,' Andrea challenged.

'Her.' Jason pointed to a sign that rose above the State Street Theater. 'Marla Winters. We're like that.' He crossed his fingers and held them up in front of her. 'I can get tickets for her show. Just name the night you want to go.'

'Marla Winters?' Andrea asked sceptically as she stared at the sign. Marla Winters, with her sultry grey-green eyes and shining silver-blonde tresses, was probably the most recognisable woman in the country, an actress who had been called 'the heir to Marilyn Monroe' by more than a few critics. She was in Boston for a benefit performance, and Andrea might have believed that Jason could get two tickets for her show, but she didn't for a minute believe that he knew the woman personally. Jason was simply bragging, and this time he'd gone too far.

'Hm,' Andrea murmured cynically. 'I'll bet you know the King of Sweden, too. I'll bet you go partridge hunting together every fall.'

'I'm serious.' Jason followed her down the street. 'Why don't you believe me?'

'I believe that you're a very gifted writer, and you would have been rich and famous by now if you had ever written some of your outrageous inventions down,' Andrea answered honestly. 'I wish you would. I believe in your talent, Jason.'

'You believe in my talent, but not in me. That's the problem, isn't it?' he asked, seizing her wrist to stop her. Then he coaxed her back against a nearby wall, leaning close to trap her there with the strength of his lean body. 'Shall we have a bet, love?' he suggested in a seductive whisper. 'I'll introduce you to Marla Winters, and your forfeit will be . . .' He paused a moment as he touched an errant auburn strand that fell across her forehead. 'You'll spend the night with me.'

It was too reckless a forfeit, Andrea knew, meeting his firm eyes with a sudden doubt. Maybe he *did* know Marla Winters. Anything was possible with Jason Dorning. 'And if I can't introduce you to her, *I'll* spend the night with *you*!' His grin was back, as impish as his laughing eyes. Andrea relaxed. This was nothing but another one of Jason's exasperating jokes. Either way, he would claim that he had won.

'Tonight?' Jason asked, brushing her cheek with a seductive kiss that raised a thoroughly unwelcomed longing. 'We could spend the night alone . . .' His mouth touched hers, then slid away, teasing her with his carefully restrained desire. 'Somewhere quiet and deserted,' he whispered as he met her mouth again. This time there was less restraint. His mouth softened over hers, entreating an answering response that she strove vainly not to give.

'Jason . . .' she murmured warily as he leaned closer to deepen the caress. But it was no use. Common sense was no defence against the longing he could raise so easily with his lingering, warm kiss. 'I'm going to a party tonight,' she objected as she pulled her mouth away. Her breath was quick and shallow, and her face was flushed to pinkness underneath his touch. 'With Robert.' She barely managed to breathe out the words.

'I'll have to find a way to change your plans.' His eyes were dark and fathomless with hunger as he held her stare. 'Won't I, love?' he asked her as his arms circled her slim waist.

'I don't think that would be a good idea, Jason,' she answered breathlessly as he pulled her closer. It had been a mistake to encourage him at all, she realised now as his thigh pressed close to hers. She was too much in love with him already, and this game they played was far too dangerous to continue. 'And I don't think you should . . .' kiss me again, she would have finished if his mouth hadn't descended to stop the words in her panic-tightened throat.

Andrea struggled only briefly in his arms before she closed her eyes and fell through a vast universe of passion. She was going to marry Robert, she tried to remind herself as Jason's mouth bore down with insistent hunger. But she didn't love him. That truth was clear enough as Jason's kisses raised her to a peak of excited longing she had never known before.

'Atta way! Yay! Not bad for old folks.' Andrea's eyes flew open at the round of applause, and even Jason seemed surprised when he realised that they weren't alone. He released his hold and turned around to stare at a crowd of enthusiastically clapping teenagers. Then his face burst wide into a grin. He held out his arms like an orchestra conductor and gave them a formal bow.

It was an act, Andrea reminded herself firmly, trying to pull her common sense around her like a cloak to ward off the dizzying confusion that had entered her life. Jason didn't want her. As soon as he got part of the estate he would leave again, and she would feel even more alone than she had felt before.

'Donations gratefully accepted,' said Jason, pulling off his hat and holding it out to the crowd. 'For the old folks' home.'

Jason didn't love her, Andrea knew, casting a quick glance at his powerful back. But if he kissed her again, she would convince herself that he had feelings he didn't possess. She pulled her coat together and slipped quietly around the corner before he had a chance to stop her.

CHAPTER FIVE

ANDREA wandered restlessly from room to room of the Pantonne estate, feeling self-conscious as Robert's friends stopped their conversations to greet her with overt surprise. Maybe she had gone too far. Her hair was curled like a brass-coloured halo around her face, and the lacy dress she wore was not at all like the sensible, subdued clothing she usually chose for herself.

'Andrea!' Robert had whispered incredulously when she had opened her apartment door. Then his eyes had searched her face with an uneasy question, but he didn't have the courage to ask why she looked so inexplicably excited.

Jason was the reason, Andrea knew, searching the crowded rooms for the sight of a smiling face and the sound of a quicksilver laugh that would thrill her senses. *His* face she understood. *His* rippling laughter of amusement. It was impossible that he would be here at one of Boston's most exclusive parties, but she looked anyway, believing in the impossible now that Jason Dorning had returned to her life.

She cared for Robert Dorning, but it wasn't the kind of love a woman would have to feel to spend a lifetime with a man. She knew that clearly now. She had argued with herself all afternoon, telling herself that Jason's manipulations were simply an attempt to blackmail his brother for part of the estate, but in the end it didn't really matter why he was doing what he did.

Her world lit up when he was with her. Even her anger and her irritation were an indication that she cared what Jason thought of her. Maybe that wasn't love, but it was too powerful to deny, and far too powerful to let her marry Robert with an easy conscience.

'My dear Andrea!' a delighted voice called out, and when she turned around she met Vincent Carpezzi's warmly appreciative old eyes. 'My dear!' He breathed the words as he reached out to seize her hand. 'Look at you! Why, I never . . .'

He stopped, breathless with admiration, and studied her smooth face. Then he lowered his voice to a conspiratorial whisper. 'I can't say I wasn't warned. When I first arrived one of my gentleman acquaintances said, "Wait until you see Andrea." Well . . . my dear,' he repeated as he patted her hand approvingly, 'I wasn't warned strongly enough. You've given my heart quite a turn now, haven't you?'

'I'm glad you approve.' Andrea rewarded his appreciation with a kiss against his cheek. 'And— I'm glad you're here,' she added, shaking herself out of the confusion she had felt all night. If she were going to extricate herself from the mess that she was in, she had better do it one step at a time. 'I'd like to talk to you about a problem.'

'Of course,' the lawyer frowned, glancing past

her shoulder to the room beyond. 'Robert's here, isn't he? He hasn't left you all alone at a party?'

'He's in the library discussing business with Albert Pantonne,' Andrea explained, slipping her arm through Vincent's to lead him to a quiet corner of the room. 'I want to discuss a legal matter,' she explained hesitantly. 'Is that all right?'

'My dear Andrea,' Vincent answered as she slipped her arm through his, 'I have one firm rule. I never discuss legal matters at a party. Unless I can discuss them with a beautiful woman. Then I talk all night.'

'I've been wondering about the legality of Creighton Dorning's will,' she started as soon as she sat down beside him. 'Do many people do it the way he did?'

'Videotaping is still relatively rare, but there are precedents,' Vincent assured her quickly. 'It's entirely proper, if that's what's worrying your pretty little head.'

'No.' Andrea couldn't help her smile. Vincent Carpezzi had treated her like a much brighter woman before he had decided that she was pretty. 'I mean the provisions themselves. Robert's inheritance is contingent on the actions of a third party, isn't it? Does that have a precedent?'

Vincent's drink stopped halfway to his lips. 'I mean,' Andrea forged on, 'if I marry Robert, he inherits. If I don't ... It wouldn't be fair if he didn't,' she explained. 'His actions haven't changed. Do you understand what I'm saying?'

'Well ... yes. Are you ...' He paused, and

Andrea understood that he was trying to frame a
personal question in the most delicate of terms.
'. . . not sure, perhaps? You were seeing Robert
when Creighton Dorning made the will. He had an
expectation that you would wish to marry Robert.'

'I know. I had that expectation, too. It's just that
. . . I seem to have got cold feet,' she admitted
honestly. 'I'm not sure I want to get married . . . Not
now. Maybe not ever. It seems like such a
permanent step to take when you're not sure of your
own feelings.'

Vincent visibly relaxed. 'All brides feel that way,
my dear.' He patted her hand reassuringly. 'So do all
grooms. I nearly bolted before all three of my
weddings. I'm surprised anybody gets married to
anybody!' He warmed to his subject. 'Nowadays,
with the divorce rate the way it is, and alimony
payments, and pre-nuptial agreements. I often
wonder how a couple makes it to the altar without
being carried there in strait-jackets. But it all works
itself out. You say, "I do," and then you're stuck to
make the best of each other,' Vincent reassured her
blithely. 'That's really the best way. Sink or swim.
Most people find a way to swim.

'But what would happen if I didn't marry
Robert?' Andrea tried to turn the subject back to
the hard facts. 'Legally, I mean. Would he lose
everything?'

'He'd continue as acting president of Dorning
Imports until such time as you *are* married.'

'And if I don't marry him?' she pressed. 'Ever?
What if I married someone else?'

'Oh.' Vincent frowned with thought. 'Well, in that case, the estate would be turned back to the courts as if there had been no will at all.'

'And?' she prompted curiously.

'And it would be divided equally among his legitimate heirs.' He stopped suddenly, as if he were embarrassed by his indiscretion. 'Legitimate being a legal term, of course,' he hastened to explain. 'There is no question that Jason Dorning is Creighton's son, so, although technically he's illegitimate, for the purposes of this discussion he's legitimate. Am I making sense to you, my dear?'

'Yes.' Andrea stared at the lawyer's kindly face. 'If I don't marry Robert, the estate will be equally divided between his two sons?'

'Less the legal expenses, of course. In a way it would be fair,' he conjectured hypothetically. 'I didn't approve of Creighton cutting Jason out like that, but I suppose he had his reasons.'

Andrea felt as if a door had opened in front of her and sunlight had flooded in to light her path. She didn't have to marry Robert! If she didn't, the estate would be divided equally, the way it should have been.

'Are you proposing to my fiancée, Vincent?' Robert's voice was drily amused as he and their hostess approached them and he laid a possessive arm across Andrea's slim shoulders.

'Oh . . .' Vincent cleared his throat uneasily. 'Well . . .'

'We were discussing a point of law,' Andrea volunteered, wondering how she was going to break the news to Robert. There was a way out of the tangled mess of her emotions, a path so wide and clear she wondered why it had caused her such an agony of indecision. She didn't have to marry anyone at all.

She would have to break the news to Robert. But not tonight, she thought, glancing upward at his smiling face and feeling one last surge of guilt.

It wouldn't be easy for him to hear the truth. His pride would be hurt, if nothing else, and she didn't delude herself that he would be as delighted as she was by the idea of fairness. Under Creighton's will, the whole estate was his. Now he would have to share it with his brother.

'What do you think of Andrea?' Janice Pantonne asked the old lawyer, who was lost in troubled thought.

'Hm?' He looked up, befuddled for a moment before he caught the train of thought. 'Oh. She's . . . Well, I've already flattered her with my opinion,' he responded warmly, rising to his feet. 'Not that the opinion of an old man matters. It's the young men who should be telling her the things she needs to hear.' At this, his eyes flickered to Robert Dorning's face as if he expected the man to understand the urgency of his suggestion. But Robert's attention had been drawn to the low buzz of excited conversation that suddenly filled the room.

'My word,' whispered Robert, catching sight of the exquisite woman who had just arrived. 'That's Marla Winters, isn't it? I didn't know you knew her, Janice.'

Andrea could do nothing more than stare. She had grown used to surprises ever since Jason had wandered back into her life, but at that moment she was gripped by the shock of a totally impossible event. Jason had told her that he knew Marla Winters, and he was producing her as proof.

'She's in Boston for a benefit performance,' Janice informed them in a squeakingly excited voice. 'I read that in the *Globe* this morning, but why . . . Oh, my! . . . Why would she come here? Do you think someone will introduce us?'

'I'm sure someone will,' Andrea predicted evenly, wondering what kind of commotion this escapade of Jason's was apt to cause.

'And who is *that?*' Janice's voice trembled with awed curiosity as Marla Winters' companion turned around and showed his face more fully. Robert straightened up so suddenly Andrea was afraid that he was going to cry out.

It was only a short moment before the new guests made their way across the crowded room to confront their hostess. 'Hi.' Marla Winters smiled with naïve apology as she held out her hand. 'This is awful of us, and it's all my fault, really. You shouldn't blame Jason because it wasn't his idea, and he didn't want to bring me here, but I insisted.'

'Oh . . . ?' Janice Pantonne answered, more confused now than she had been before.

'You see, we were passing by,' Marla continued in a girlish voice. 'And Jason mentioned that the people who lived here were very interesting. And then he mentioned that they were having a party tonight, so I said, "Let's go to their party." But Jason said, "Marla, love, I haven't been invited. I haven't seen these people in ten years." But I insisted that we come to the door and ask. It was terrible of me, really. Do you mind?'

'Oh . . .' Janice murmured, completely over-whelmed now by Marla's sweetly delivered apology. 'I loved your last movie, *Destiny's Deliverance*. Just—loved it.'

Andrea met Jason's eyes with more than a little curiosity, trying to decipher the look that lingered on his handsome features. Triumph. That was clear enough. He had the look of a man who had been holding a secret ace and thoroughly enjoyed his chance to play it, but it was more than that. There was a wilful stubbornness in his dark eyes when he cast a glance at Andrea and then at the man who held his arm so casually around her.

'Robert.' He greeted his brother with a cordial nod.

'Jason.'

Then Jason turned his attention to the others. 'Janice Pantonne, this is Marla Winters.'

'I know . . .'

'I don't know if you remember me.' He held out his hand. 'I'm Jason Dorning. We met years ago.'

'Of course,' Janice nodded breathlessly. 'I've always wondered what became of you.'

'Vincent Carpezzi,' Jason continued with the introductions. 'Vincent is one of the finest lawyers in Boston.'

'How nice.' Marla's smile was genuine. 'I like

lawyers. They've saved my life more than once. And so has Jason, of course. That's how we met. He *really* saved my life.'

'They're not interested in that, love,' Jason admonished the woman gently. *Au contraire*, Andrea thought, studying the sweet tableau. How Jason had saved Marla Winters' life was only one of the things she would like to hear far more about.

'My brother, Robert.'

'I didn't know you had a brother.'

'Well, I do,' Jason answered simply, meeting Robert's eyes with a full stare of challenge. 'Don't I?' Robert didn't answer.

'Hi.' Marla held out her hand to break the painful silence, and Robert had the grace to take it.

'And Andrea McKinley,' Jason redirected the course of the introductions. What came next was not what Andrea expected.

'Are you Andy?' Marla was openly delighted. 'Jason says you do spells and things, you know, like magic. I hope you're not going to turn me into a frog.'

'She doesn't do frog-spells,' Jason answered. 'Andy specialises in block-of-ice incantations.'

'Oh.' Marla looked up anxiously at Jason's face, and then relaxed. 'I don't always know when he's teasing me,' she explained, meeting Andrea's eyes with open confidence.

Andrea's mouth twitched upward as she noted Jason's grin. 'We all have that trouble with Jason,' she assured her evenly.

'And last, but surely not least ——' Jason turned

Marla to face the stiff-spined man who had joined their group. 'Marla Winters, this is Albert Pantonne. Maybe you should repeat your pretty little apology about crashing his party before he remembers that he never liked me.'

'It's all my fault,' Marla repeated obediently as she held out her hand. 'If we're not welcome, we'll go away.'

'Of course they're welcome,' Janice answered quickly. 'Isn't that right, Albert?'

Albert Pantonne glanced at his wife's hopefully flushed features, then at the other guests who watched with open interest. He could do nothing but relent and welcome them to stay.

Marla Winters wasn't stupid. That was one of the few facts that Andrea was sure of in the addled, upside-down situation Jason had created. She was warm and friendly, and she possessed an honest sweetness that was apparent in the directness of her grey-green eyes. But she wasn't half as dumb as she made herself out to be.

And neither was Jason. If he was trying to romance his brother's fiancée, he wouldn't have shown up at a party with a woman like Marla Winters. Maybe he was trying to make her jealous, Andrea conjectured as she sipped the last of her champagne and watched the pretty woman hold court with at least a dozen men. No, that wasn't it, she knew instinctively. Using Marla Winters to make Andrea McKinley jealous would have been like shooting a sparrow with a cannon. Jason was far too bright for that.

'Where's your bodyguard?'

Andrea smiled at the sound of the low, throaty voice. She had expected Jason to seek her out eventually. 'He's locked in the library with Albert Pantonne. They're laying strategy, I suspect.'

'Oh?' Jason leaned back against the wall. 'Are the barbarians attacking?'

Andrea didn't try to hide her laugh. 'They've stormed the parapets,' she admitted a little drunkenly. Jason met her eyes with appreciative curiosity. She was being brash and openly flirtatious. Reckless was the word that came most quickly to her mind as she met his deep, brown eyes. This man made her believe in recklessness, and if she wasn't careful, he could make her believe in love as well. 'I like you, Jason,' she admitted honestly. 'I always have.'

His mouth lurched upward in a grin, but when he reached out to touch her, she quickly backed away. 'Patience,' she admonished. 'You know all about patience, don't you?'

'What do you mean by that?'

'I mean that you're a very clever man. But you're crazy if you think I'm going to spend the night with you. You're far too attractive, and I don't trust myself enough.' She took another glass of champagne from a nearby table. 'I don't trust you, either, by the way, so that makes us even.'

'I like intelligent women, Andy,' he murmured seductively beside her ear. 'Intelligent, beautiful women are even more of a treat.'

'That's why you like Marla Winters.' She said it so matter-of-factly that Jason smiled again.

'She'll be pleased to hear that you think she's intelligent. Very few people understand that.'

'Oh, I understand it,' Andrea agreed. 'She's also a very gifted actress, and I think . . .' She met Jason's eyes for confirmation. 'I think she's a nice woman. I can't help liking her.'

'Good.' Jason seemed relieved. 'Marla and I have a special kind of friendship. Take a party like this, for instance. If we come together, we don't necessarily have to leave together.'

'I see.' His meaning wasn't all that subtle. 'Who do you think Marla will leave with tonight?'

'It depends on who I leave with,' Jason answered casually, but there was nothing casual in the eyes that touched her face like a caress, eliciting a trembling excitement.

'Ah.' She smiled just slightly, enjoying her new-found ability to tease him. She would have left with him this minute if there weren't other consider-ations, but she wasn't going to admit that to him quite so easily. Let him work for his flirtation. She remembered his comments about her ability to turn him to a block of ice and decided to try that exercise instead. Wordlessly she fixed him with her eyes, studying his face until she knew every line and angle of his tanned, handsome features.

'Are you going to leave with me?' he demanded, losing patience first.

'I can't,' she answered simply. 'I came with someone else.'

'So did I.'

'But Robert and I don't have such a casual arrangement,' she reminded him. 'Robert and I happen to be engaged.'

He said nothing in reply, although he was far from pleased. Neither of them spoke for several minutes. They stood side by side, intensely aware of each other's closeness as they watched the couples move like coloured shadows to the soft, romantic music of the violins.

'I have something important to ask you,' Jason confided in a whisper.

'About your manuscript?'

'No,' he answered, snaking his arm around her waist to coax her towards the french doors. 'Let's talk on the terrace. It's too personal to discuss in here.'

'I'll bet it is,' laughed Andrea. Then, a moment later, she sucked in her breath. The air outside was as cold as sea water against her warm, flushed skin. 'Brrrr!' she shivered, turning back, only to find that he had blocked the way. 'I'm going to catch pneumonia out here,' she said seriously, but Jason stripped off his jacket and wrapped it around her trembling shoulders.

'Now *you're* going to catch pneumonia,' she objected as his hands spread out against her shoulders and he coaxed her back into the darkest shadows. 'In all those romantic novels where the hero and the heroine meet on the terrace, it's never thirty-two degrees. I think we should go back inside,' she suggested practically, but Jason had no intention of giving up so easily.

'I'll keep you warm,' he promised, slipping his arms around her to lead her into the steps of a slow waltz. 'I'll take you to Paradise if you let me.'

'Paradise?' Andrea asked. She had been so relieved to know she didn't have to marry Robert, and then she had drunk too much champagne, but she didn't think the champagne was responsible for her light-headed sense of pleasure as he coaxed her close. 'Humility isn't one of your problems, is it?'

'I know what I am, Andy.' His warm breath grazed her neck like a soft touch, and then he pulled away just enough to meet her soft blue eyes. 'Leave the party with me, and I'll show you what I am.'

His eyes were so warmly seductive Andrea lost herself there for a moment, realising only slowly that they had stopped and that Jason's hand had fanned out against the nape of her long neck to hold her captive to the kiss she knew would come.

'I can't leave with you,' she whispered feebly, sorry now that she had led him on. 'Robert would be humiliated.'

'Damn Robert!' Jason answered fiercely. 'You don't love him, Andy. You wouldn't be out here with me if you did. When will you admit that? Look at you,' he whispered, letting his fingertips move down possessively across her auburn curls and then across her cheek. 'Your hair, your dress . . . You did this for me, didn't you?' he insisted softly. 'You knew I'd come for you, and that's exactly what you wanted. I can see it in your eyes.'

'I don't know how I feel any more,' she answered

honestly. She closed her eyes and laid her forehead against his shoulder, silently pleading for him to give her time to know her own emotions. Her love for Jason Dorning had come too suddenly for her to trust her own reckless passion, but every time she saw him she knew that they were moving closer to the inevitable satisfaction of desire.

This man had always been her fate. She had understood that ten years ago, but now the steps were out of order. First she had to break her engagement to his brother. Then, and only then, would she be free to go to Jason Dorning.

'Leave with me, angel,' he insisted, stepping sideways to pull her down beside him on a marble bench, but in the darkness he misjudged the distance and stepped roughly on her foot.

'Ahhh.' Andrea jumped backward and lifted her wounded foot to knead it with her fingers.

'Are you hurt?' Jason's voice was suddenly concerned.

'It's okay,' she reassured him, waving aside his hand as she eased herself down to the bench and slipped off her shoe. 'My feet have been stepped on before.'

'You do it all the time, right?' Jason asked as he knelt down in front of her and balanced her foot against his knee. 'Maybe I broke it,' he suggested as he massaged her arch in wide, smooth circles with his fingertips.

'You didn't break it.'

'You can't always tell,' he cautioned. 'I worked with a man who broke his foot and didn't know it. It healed sideways and he's got arthritis to this day.'

Andrea couldn't help her laugh. 'My foot isn't broken, Jason.'

'He tells the weather by it,' he continued. 'The TV station in Anaheim calls him up to see if it's going to rain. Does this hurt?' He dug his thumb into her flesh and twisted it until she yelped with pain. 'It's broken,' he decided, standing up abruptly. 'I've got to get you to a hospital right away.'

'What?'

Before she could object, Jason had lifted her like a child in his strong arms. 'Oops! Let's not forget this.' He stopped only long enough to collect her shoe, then he carried her down the terrace steps to the gravel driveway.

'It's not broken, Jason. Let me go!' She struck her fist against his shoulder, but nothing stopped him. 'I'm serious, Jason! My foot is *not* broken! It doesn't even hurt now.' He opened the door of a small red sports car and deposited her on the seat, hurrying around to slide into the driver's side before she could escape.

'Don't panic,' he said calmly as he turned a key in the ignition and they bucked forward with a grinding complaint of gears. 'I'm going to take you to an emergency room to see about that foot. It's the least I can do after breaking it like that.'

'It's not . . .' Andrea stopped as another, far worse thought occurred to her. 'You're not stealing this car, are you?'

'No, it's Marla's.'

'How is Marla going to get home?' she demanded

as he manoeuvred the car out on to the open
highway. She didn't for a minute think that they
were bound for a hospital, or that Jason planned to
return her to the arms of her fiancé when his little
spree was finished.

'She'll get a ride from someone. Robert maybe.'

'Oh.' So that was it, she realised. Marla and Jason
had cooked up a convenient plot to snatch her.
'Robert's going to be furious,' she warned him. 'He
might even have the police arrest you.'

'On what grounds?'

'Kidnapping.'

'Wouldn't that be a kick in the teeth?' Jason
muttered, although he didn't seem the least bit
worried. 'A guy rushes a woman to the hospital for
emergency treatment, and he gets himself arrested
for a major crime. No wonder people don't stop to
help any more. No one gets involved. It's a shame.
It really is.'

'You're being an idiot,' laughed Andrea. 'You're
kidnapping me, and I know that you're kidnapping
me.'

'I know that you know that I know that you know
I'm kidnapping you,' he answered facetiously,
casting her a sidelong glance. 'How come you look
so excited, love?'

'I'm not.' She leaned back against the seat, and
pulled his jacket more securely around her. It
smelled like him, she thought, losing herself for just
a moment in the musky-sweet aroma of his skin.
She *was* excited, she admitted to herself. He had
stormed the defences of the castle, and now he was

carrying her away like a Sabine to make her his docile, willing slave.

That was rubbish. She shook her head impatiently, and tried desperately to think. He was undermining her right to make her own decisions. Negating her dignity as a woman. Forcing his whims down her throat. Not to mention causing her all kinds of trouble with Robert later. It would have been hard enough to tell Robert that she couldn't marry him before this stupid stunt. Now Robert would probably have apoplexy when he heard the news!

'You *look* excited,' Jason pressed the point.

'And you look like a horse's ass,' she retorted, even more irritated when he laughed.

CHAPTER SIX

'WHAT are we doing *here*?' Andrea demanded half an hour later when Jason pulled into a hospital car park and turned off the engine.

'Getting your broken foot attended to,' he answered, slamming his door behind him and walking around the car to open hers. 'Maybe we should ask the doctor about that memory problem of yours, too.'

'I don't have a broken foot,' she reminded him as he stooped down to whisk her off her feet. 'A joke is a joke, Jason,' she cautioned. 'But sometimes it's necessary to know when the joke has gone far enough. Like now. Do you hear me, Jason?' She banged her shoe against his back, but she already knew her protests were in vain. Jason didn't march to his own drummer. He had a whole imaginary band.

'We're going to look like imbeciles,' she moaned as he carried her to the emergency room entrance. 'My foot isn't broken, Jason.'

'I broke her foot,' Jason announced as he carried her to the desk in the brightly-lit foyer of the emergency room.

'He didn't break my foot,' Andrea renewed her protest as she squirmed in his strong arms. No matter how she tried, she couldn't wriggle out of

Jason's determined grasp.

'She's hysterical, too,' he explained, holding her with a gentle determination to stop her useless struggles. 'She hates doctors. She's had a morbid fear of them ever since her grandmother went to the hospital and never returned. She was seven then. Bad age to lose someone, especially someone like Nana McKinley.'

'I never even knew my grandmother!'

'See what I mean?' Jason suggested with a look of desperate concern. 'She's blanked it out completely. But right now the trouble is her foot. There was a snap, like a twig breaking, and then she was hobbling around.'

'It's not broken . . .' Andrea's words were a moan as she pressed her face against Jason's shoulder. She was either going to cry or laugh. Either one would be appropriate for this ridiculous situation.

'Insurance?' The nurse set a sheaf of papers on the counter.

'No insurance,' Jason answered, freeing one hand just enouqh to find a wallet in his pocket. 'I've got a credit card, though. Do you take American Express?'

She was going to laugh. Andrea drove her face hard against his neck, but even that wasn't enough to stifle her sudden amusement at the situation.

'There now, love,' he murmured, soothing her with his hand. 'Try to stay in control.'

'Is she going to be all right?' the nurse demanded. 'We can use restraints.'

'No!' Jason answered with merciful determination. 'As long as I'm with her, she's all right. Aren't you, Andy?'

'Yes.' She gave a strangled answer, then dissolved into a laugh again.

'Is this is your current address?' the nurse was asking. 'Post office box one-five-seven, Green Harbor, Maine?'

'Yep.'

'I see . . . And your name is Dorning? D-O-R-N-I-N-G?'

'That's right. Could we move along?' he asked, heaving Andrea a little higher against his chest. 'She's not as light as she looks.'

Andrea lay on the examination table and counted the tiny rows of dots in the stained acoustic tile above her head while she waited for Jason to return. She had decided to be calm. The mention of restraints had convinced her that she'd be better off to go along with Jason's merry little game. If she insisted on the truth she would end up in a padded cell, or Jason would be carted off and, despite her exasperation, she didn't want that, either.

'Did you tell them that I eat worms for breakfast?' she demanded when she heard the door open and shut behind her.

'Good God! Do you?'

'Oh!' Andrea turned just far enough to see a doctor in a white, starched lab coat, carrying her chart. 'I thought you were Jason. No, I don't eat worms. And my foot isn't broken, either.'

'You're right,' the grey-haired man agreed good-

naturedly, coming around the table to take her foot
in the palm of his warm hand. 'Your X-rays show no
sign of damage. Just relax a minute. I'm going to
wiggle your foot around to see if you've got a
sprain.'

Andrea relaxed while he bent her foot up and
down and moved it in a circle. 'Your husband is
very devoted to your welfare, isn't he?'

'My . . .' She lifted her head to stare at the
physician. This pack of lies had gone quite far
enough already. Now he was claiming to be her
husband, too? She almost snapped a denial, but she
thought better of her anger and laid her head back
down. The best course of action was to go along
with Jason's lies and settle with him later. 'Jason is
extremely devoted,' she agreed. 'Sometimes I wish
he were a little less attentive.'

'Is that the problem? That you feel he's too
demanding? Does this hurt?'

'No.' Andrea stared at the ceiling trying to
decipher the meaning of the doctor's words.

'This?' He twisted her foot over to the side.

'No.'

'Well, it's not a sprain or strain,' the doctor
announced cheerfuly. 'I suspect that you're a
perfectly healthy woman, Mrs Dorning. You have a
devoted, loving husband. He's out in the hallway
right now calling your brother Robert to reassure
him.'

'He is?' Andrea asked, wondering what mischief
Jason was up to now. And what he had been up to
for the past half hour. The doctor eased himself

back against the counter and crossed his arms in an attitude that she recognised from her childhood. She was about to get a lecture.

'Marital adjustment is still a bigger problem than people think,' he started in a kindly voice. 'Despite the recent revolution in sexual mores, many women are still frightened by what they see as the brutal hungers of a total stranger.' Andrea stared numbly at the doctor's face, wondering what on earth he expected her to say.

'But your husband isn't a total stranger, is he?'

'No.' She managed to get out the word in a strangled whisper.

'Of course he isn't,' the man smiled kindly. 'He's a flesh and blood human being who cares very deeply for you. And the kind of . . .' the doctor faltered for a word that wouldn't frighten her, '. . . "communication" he wants with you is only normal for a healthy man. Will you try to remember that, Mrs Dorning?'

'I'll remember,' she promised evenly. 'I'll communicate with my husband as soon as we're alone.'

'Good girl.' He gave her a reassuring pat on the shoulder, then looked up just as the door was opened. 'Ah, Mr Dorning, come in. Your wife is fit and healthy, and she's ready to go home now.'

'Great,' Jason grinned, but his grin faded as he glanced at Andrea and met her fiery violet eyes. 'Well . . . Good, good, good,' he murmured, glancing around the room until he found his jacket. 'Shall we be on our way, love?'

'Whatever you say, sugarcake.' She bit out the

words as she buckled her shoe and slid down from the table. A minute later she was striding down the hallway with Jason Dorning following as best he could.

'What happened in there?' he demanded when they reached the car. 'The doctor didn't hurt you, did he?'

'No!' She slammed the door in Jason's face and sank down on the seat.

He came around the front and slid into the driver's seat with a nervous glance in her direction. 'So? Are you going to tell me or not?'

'Sure, I'll tell you,' Andrea agreed. 'The doctor gave me a lecture about my sexual problems. He seems to think I'm a trembling little maiden who is frightened by my husband's barbaric hungers. Where do you think he got that idea, Jason?' she demanded furiously.

'Oh . . .'Jason's answer was a groan. 'That was my fault,' he confessed. 'But I did it for you, love.' Andrea glared at him so coldly he gave her a sheepishly apologetic smile. 'He looked at the notes the nurse had written on your chart, and he said, "Why don't we give your wife a sedative?" Then, I'm afraid, I said something stupid.'

'I believe it,' Andrea snapped. 'What exactly did you say?'

'Well . . .' he hesitated, 'I said, "Good lord, don't knock her out. I have enough trouble getting her into bed as it is."'

Andrea couldn't help her smile. It was the kind of flip remark that Jason was used to making, the kind of remark a concerned doctor could easily misunderstand. 'Oh!' She clapped her hand against her mouth to stop her laugh. 'I think I'm going crazy,' she admitted. 'I'd have to be crazy to find this situation funny!'

Jason's face lifted into a beaming, boyish grin that was altogether too seductive. 'You still like me, don't you, Andy?'

'Yes,' she admitted honestly as she laid her cheek against the cushion and regarded his handsome, impish face. 'I still like you. Far too much for my own good.'

'Good,' he whispered as he turned the key in the ignition and backed the small red sports car out of the parking space. 'For a minute, I thought I'd gone too far.'

They were travelling north, Andrea realised, reading the exit signs on Route One-two-eight. North, away from Boston. Why didn't that surprise her?

Nothing about Jason could surprise her any more, she thought philosophically, turning her head enough to watch the man who drove with an easy sense of self-assurance. 'What did you tell Robert?' she asked curiously, remembering his phone call.

'I didn't talk to him. I had to leave a message with the maid.'

'And?'

'And I said you'd hurt your foot,' Jason answered matter-of-factly. 'I took you to a hospital to have it X-rayed. It's all right. Don't wait up. I'll take you home. Something along those lines.'

'I see,' she smiled, beginning to understand how Jason's mind worked. He hadn't told Robert which hospital, of course. It would take Robert half the night to call every emergency room in the Boston area. Then there was the matter of her name. They had 'accidentally' listed her as Andrea Dorning because Jason had given the impression that she was his wife. That would cause delays.

Even this aimless driving through the wintry night could be explained away. She had been hysterical at the hospital. Jason was driving her around to calm her down, oblivious to the fact that people would be worried. After all, he had reassured them that he would see her home. Every part of his plot could be seen as innocent if Robert decided to report him to the police. The only person who could shed a different light on the events liked him too much to get him into trouble.

'You'd make a great criminal, Jason,' Andrea complimented sleepily.

'Thank you, love. I've always thought so.'

She drifted into a peaceful half sleep, no longer caring where she was or where this strange odyssey was takinq her. She trusted Jason not to hurt her, and that was all she had to know.

She felt the car slow, then stop, and squinted her eyes at a barrage of pink neon light, but she barely had time to contemplate the brightly-lit Dunkin' Donuts sign before Jason was back in the car with a large thermos and a box.

A few moments later, the car stopped again. She heard Jason rummage in the boot, and saw him disappear into the darkness, piled like a packhorse with blankets and pillows. Then he was back, opening the door and shaking her slim shoulder to rouse her from her sleep. 'Put on my sheepskin coat,' he suggested as he pulled her to her feet in the chill, bracing air. 'I'll wear the jacket.'

'Where are we?' Andrea asked, squinting into the darkness that surrounded them. Above their heads a billion stars twinkled with cold light, and she could hear a distant splash of surf.

'Good Harbor Beach in Gloucester.'

'Of course,' she murmured as he lifted her against his chest and carried her across the dunes, closer and closer to the soft, melodic thunder of the sea. 'A beach, in the dead of night, in the middle of December. I should have thought of this myself.' She felt the chuckle in his throat and pressed her face against it, as trustingly compliant as a little girl swept up in strong, warm arms.

He set her down on a bed of down-filled quilts, then sat behind her and pulled the other quilts around them until they were safely hidden in a cave of fragrant warmth. 'The coffee's light on the cream and sugar. I hope you like it that way.' He reached around her to unscrew the cap and poured some of the steaming liquid into the cup that comprised a lid. 'We'll have to share the cup.'

A cupful of the heady, steaming coffee revived Andrea's groggy senses and she leaned back against him, inhaling the musky sweetness of his skin as it intermingled with the sharp salt aroma of the sea. They might have been the only people in the universe, she thought, gazing out into the liquid blackness that met the moonless sky without a seam. If they were the only people in the universe, he'd be enough for her, she knew.

Presently, she stirred and poured a second cup of coffee. 'A thermos, half a dozen quilts ... One might suspect that you and Marla had this planned.'

'Hm,' he answered lazily.

'What did you do for Marla?' Andrea asked curiously as she handed him the cup. 'How did you *really* save her life?'

'Do you remember that book she wrote six years ago? *Lost Out Here In The Stars*?'

'Yes. I read it.' It was written in Marla's breathlessly naïve tone, but it had been a well-constructed book, and thoroughly enjoyable. 'It was surprisingly well written.'

'Thank you.'

She turned just enough to meet his eyes. 'You wrote Marla's book?'

'Yep.' He took a sip of coffee and handed the cup back. 'Marla was bright enough to realise that the book she had committed herself to write was a mess. Her editor had a friend who had a friend who might be able to pull it all together.' He shrugged self-effacingly. 'That's how I met Marla. We've been friends ever since.'

'Friends and ...'

'Nope.' His answer was so quick Andrea smiled. That was exactly what she had meant to ask. 'I didn't jump into bed with her while we were writing the book because I know trouble when I see it coming. By the time we had finished the book, we knew each other so well we might as well have been brother and sister,' Jason explained matter-of-factly. 'To me, she's Sally Lissack from Detroit, not a sex goddess any man would kill himself to have. I think Marla's grateful that I see her that way.'

'And me?' asked Andrea wondering if he saw her as a sister, too. 'Am I still a skinny-legged teenager from Boston?'

'You know you're not.'

That was all he said, but the simplicity of the answer thrilled her because it seemed to come from a quiet self-assurance deep inside his heart. When he put his arm around her, she leaned back peacefully against his chest. 'When are you going to let me see your novel, Jason?'

'Some day,' he answered her evasively. 'Someday I'll let you see it all.'

'There's more than one?' she squirmed around to see his face. He had had such talent once. Even at fifteen she had understood the power of his dramatically vivid imagination, and she had always expected to see his name on a best-selling novel. But she never had.

'Change the subject,' he commanded, leaning down to lightly touch his mouth to hers. 'I didn't bring you here to talk about my writing.'

'Why did you, then?'

'Just to be with you for a little while,' he answered with every evidence of honesty. 'Away from all the things I can't compete with.'

They didn't talk at all for a long time. Andrea lay

easily in the crook of Jason's arm, her cheek pressed to his hard chest where she could hear the rhythmic pounding of his heart. There was something melancholy about the sound. The charming clown was gone, and here, she sensed, was the real Jason Dorning, proud and lonely, battered but unbowed.

'Dawn is coming.' He broke their silence finally. Andrea gazed up at the darkened sky, studying the velvet vault set with a million stars. Where was the dawn? she wondered, meeting his eyes with a silent question.

'Don't you feel it?' he asked with a smile. 'The air is softer, the stars a little duller. The blackness of the sky is luminescent.' She looked and saw all that, just as Jason had described it. A moment later a bird call warbled in the air to confirm his intuition.

'When I was a kid I thought that the end of night was pasted to the beginning of the day to make it all a circle. That makes this time of day the seam of time,' Jason continued in a melancholy voice, as if he were talking to himself, not her. 'It's the one time of day when a man knows himself the best, and can't hide from his own secrets, no matter how he tries.'

He still held her cradled in his arms and she reached up to touch his sad-eyed face. 'What do you know about yourself, Jason?' she asked curiously.

'I know that I'm lonely,' he admitted with an honesty that tore at her love-filled heart. 'I was born outside of all the circles that would have kept me warm, and I'm still outside looking in. My own brother hates the sight of me, and my father never really wanted me. He wanted a carbon copy of himself, and I couldn't be that.'

'You scare your brother,' Andrea explained. She pressed her cheek against his shoulder, trying to find words that would reach the bitter boy who still lived too painfully caught up in a past he couldn't change. 'And your father loved you very much,' she said softly as she touched her fingers to his tense, unhappy face. 'He told me once that his only regret in life was never having known his youngest son.'

Jason didn't cry, although she sensed that he was on the edge and held himself back with the force of will because he didn't want to show her what he considered weakness. She didn't push him past the point of crumpled pride. She clung to him instead, giving him a wordless comfort with the closeness of her body.

She didn't know how long they sat like that, their arms holding fast, and their bodies intertwined so firmly that she could feel the throbbing echo of each painful memory, but when he stirred at last she saw that the sky had lightened to an opalescent pearl-grey screen that told them night had ended.

Jason met her eyes with a melancholy gratitude as his hands cradled her slim face and lifted it to his. His mouth touched hers with a caress so gentle and so tender it felt like the whisper of a freshening morning breeze.

Then his hands softened to release her and he looked away, studying the frothy foam of water that sent fingers up the trackless expanse of sand. 'I'll take you home now,' he decided. 'There is something I have to do today.'

CHAPTER SEVEN

ANDREA woke from an exhausted sleep, squinting at the golden light that flowed like syrup through her bedroom window and tried to remember what had roused her. The phone, she realised with a start. The phone was jangling in the other room, screaming so insistently she knew the ringing wouldn't stop if she rolled over and buried her head beneath the pillows. She grabbed her bathrobe from the bottom of the bed and stumbled into the living room.

'Hello?' she answered with a half-stifled yawn as she balanced the receiver against her neck.

'Andrea?' The masculine voice was sharp with anger. 'Are you all right?'

'Robert?' She had forgotten him completely! 'Yes, I'm fine,' she reassured him quickly. 'You got Jason's message last night, didn't you?'

'I got his message loud and clear,' Robert snapped. 'Did he hurt you?'

'No.' She tried to keep her voice calm and even while she pulled on her robe. She hadn't expected Robert to be pleased, but there was a determined fury in his voice that made her wary for Jason's safety. 'He stepped on my foot, and we thought it might be broken, so he took me to an emergency room to have it X-rayed.' She didn't pause to

wonder why she had so easily slipped into defend
ing Jason's lies. That seemed only natural now. 'But
it was all right. Then we went somewhere for coffee,
and he brought me home. Did Marla get back to her
hotel all right?' she changed the subject hastily.
'Jason was concerned about that.'

'I'll bet he was. I took Marla Winters to her
hotel.'

'Ah.' Andrea couldn't help her smile. Only
Robert Dorning could make the privilege of being
alone with Marla Winters sound like a ghastly
chore. 'She must have liked you, then.'

'The woman was trying to waste my time. I
wasn't born yesterday, Andrea. And neither were
you,' he added sternly.

Oh, but I was, Robert, she thought wearily,
sinking down against the cushions of the couch and
pushing her curls back with a hurried hand. Her
hair still felt so strange against her cheek. It felt as
soft and caressing as Jason Dorning's hand.

She was in love, Andrea realised. With the wrong
man, at the wrong time, but it *was* love. There was
no other way to explain the soaring flights of
exhilaration whenever Jason held her close.

'We have to talk, Robert,' she suggested, knowing that she had let the situation continue far too
long already. She couldn't marry Robert because
she was in love with his brother Jason. 'I wanted to
wait for a good time to tell you, but . . .'

'No!' He answered sharply, as if he had already
guessed the truth. 'Don't say anything you'll regret.'

'I already regret not telling you the way I feel. I

can't marry . . .'

'Don't!' His voice rose with a pathetic fear. 'Not over the phone, Andrea. A woman doesn't end everything with a phone call, not if she cares about a man.'

'All right,' she agreed wearily. He was right about that much. She owed him the courtesy of telling him in person. 'Can I see you this afternoon?'

'No. I won't be here. I . . .' Robert faltered. 'Damn it, Andrea!' he cried. 'Jason has done this to us. He hates me! He's always hated me!'

'We have to talk about it, Robert.' She was close to tears now as she carried the phone to the kitchen counter and plugged in the coffee pot. It was one-thirty in the afternoon, she realised, glancing at the clock with some surprise. 'It isn't just Jason. I'm not sure you would have proposed to me if your father hadn't forced the issue with his will, and that's no reason to get married. I know this complicates the inheritance, but you'll still get half of the estate.'

'Don't!' Robert pleaded desperately. 'Don't say any more until I've had a chance to talk to you in person! I'm going to see someone in New York . . . a private detective who's very discreet and very efficient,' he blurted out before she could continue. 'I'll be back tomorrow, and then we'll know . . .'

'Know?' Andrea echoed, confused. 'Know what?'

'About Jason. I'll have the man dig up everything he can find about my brother, then you'll know what he's been doing for the past ten years.'

'You're going to have your own brother investigated?' she put in coldly. 'That's the most disgusting
thing I've ever . . .'

'Just calm down,' Robert interrupted weakly. 'I
think you should come to your senses once and for
all, Andrea . . .'

'What about *you* coming to your senses?' she
demanded furiously. 'Would it hurt you to actually
talk to your own brother? He wants you to like him!
Do you realise that?'

'He wants money, Andrea!' Robert snapped
impatiently. '*My* money.!'

'Has he asked for money?' She meant her tone to
be challengingly defiant, but there was too much
question in her own mind for her to be completely
self-assured. Would Jason go away now if Robert
gave him money?

'No,' Robert admitted slowly. 'I offered, but
he . . .'

'He turned you down?' Andrea prompted hopefully. 'What did he say?'

'He told me not to be an ass,' he admitted
honestly. 'But all that means is that he wants more
than I was willing to offer him. I'm going to have
him investigated. Now don't start yelling again,' he
cautioned quickly. 'If there's nothing in his past, I'll
be the first to apologise. And if there is . . . Either
way, the truth is the truth, Andrea. I just want you
to delay any decision you might make until we know
for certain.'

'All right,' she agreed, forcing herself to be calm.
'I know you're going to waste your money on a wild

goose chase, but it's your money. Go ahead and waste it.'

'I'll see you when I get back?'

'Yes,' she answered stiffly.

'Andrea, I . . .' Robert faltered uncomfortably for words. 'I'll see you when I get back from New York City,' he finished painfully. 'Goodbye.'

'Goodbye,' she echoed his last word as she set the phone down on its cradle with an angry thud.

Andrea's boots crunched on the frost-covered ground, and her puffs of breath hung in the air like clouds as she made her way along the cemetery path. She had wanted to bring fresh flowers to Creighton Dorning's grave, but it would have been a foolish gesture. The flowers would have wilted in the cold before she had a chance to place them on his grave. She had brought three silk roses instead, and as she climbed the sloping incline towards his grave the roses rustled like a whisper against her camel coat.

The sky was a metallic silver-grey that promised to spit snowflakes before the day had ended, and the gloomy half-light had worked on her troubled thoughts, twisting them around one way and then another until she had sought refuge from the bustle of the city. There was nothing in Jason's past that could change her mind about him, she told herself without complete conviction.

He had been gone for ten long years. What could a man do with that long a stretch of time? Write? Work? Get married and have children? Lie, cheat,

steal and murder? No! She turned her thoughts
deliberately away from the dark possibilities of her
imagination. He had been writing. He had told her
that himself. And he had travelled. With what
money?

With the money from ghost-writing Marla's
book, she reminded herself impatiently, hating
herself for the suspicions that wouldn't go away.
Robert's investigation would find nothing because
there was nothing in Jason's past to find. She had
only to listen to her heart. That told her all she had
to know.

She reached the looming Roberts monument and
stopped, surprised by the scene that waited farther
down the path. A man in a sheepskin coat stood
silently before a gravestone, his shoulders hunched
in private misery. It was Jason Dorning, Andrea
realised, unwilling to interrupt the privacy of his
grief. She stepped back until she was hidden from
his view and leaned her back against the cold
marble of the monument to wait.

Time seemed as frozen as the ground that
stretched between them, but finally he stirred and
reached his hand towards the grey stone. Andrea
couldn't read the inscription in the dim, fading
light, but she knew the words and saw them in her
mind as Jason's fingers followed the chiselled
letters. Creighton Samuel Dorning. Gone But Not
Forgotten.

'Gone but just now found' might have been more
apt. Jason's wall of bitterness had crumpled, but it
had come too late for both of them, Andrea thought,

trying to hold back tears of sympathetic regret for both the Dorning men. Jason's bitterly held defences had been released at last, but Creighton wasn't here to know his son.

Andrea was so lost in thought she didn't hear Jason's footsteps on the icy ground until too late. He was only a few yards away when he looked up and saw her, too.

His face was wet with tears, and when he realised she had seen that, he glanced restlessly away, embarrassed that she had seen his pain. 'Excuse me,' Jason muttered. He turned away abruptly and followed the path back to the tarmac road.

Half an hour later, Andrea saw the man she had been watching for, walking with his even, striding gait along the side of the highway that led into Boston. She pulled to the shoulder of the road ahead of him and leaned across to open up the door. 'Are you all right?' she asked, studying his grim, unsmiling face. All traces of the tears were gone, but there was a bleak unhappiness in his dark eyes. 'Get in,' she ordered tersely, and to her surprise he obeyed with only the slightest hesitation.

'We might as well get it over with,' Andrea said as she eased the car back into traffic. 'I know you were crying, and I don't think you're less of a man for it. "He condemned himself to cry forever in his heart because he wouldn't show the mocking world his tears." ' She quoted a passsage from Creighton Dorning's favourite novel. ' "Thus was manhood dearly bought, and comfort sorely lost." '

Jason looked up sharply, and for a moment he seemed incapable of speech. Then he lit a cigarette and blew a long, sighing stream of smoke into the air. 'What the hell is that from?' he demanded curtly.

'*Farther Now From Home*, by Joseph Dalton.' She chanced a sidelong glance in his direction, but Jason was staring fixedly out of the window as if he sought answers in the dried grasses of the weed-choked fields. 'It was your father's favourite book. He was reading it when he died.'

'Pretty classy reading for the old man, wasn't it?' he muttered through clenched teeth. 'I thought he was a Jarvis Drew fan.'

Andrea didn't answer his bitter comment. She didn't doubt the pain that he still felt, and she couldn't change the past. All she could offer him was a sympathetic friendship. 'Where would you like me to take you, Jason?'

'I'd like you to take me home with you,' he answered with blunt honesty. 'But you'd be asking for trouble if you did.'

They would make love. Andrea understood his warning. Every touch and every dark-eyed glance had been leading to that moment when Jason would take her in his arms and satisfy a longing that had been born ten long years before.

And afterwards ... What would happen then? she wondered. Would he go away again? Or would he stay beside her, returning the love that she was willing to give him? It didn't matter, she realised, casting a sidelong glance at Jason's still, tense face.

She wanted him so much she didn't care about the future and useless guarantees of love.

'Finding a parking space is considered a good omen in this city,' Andrea made nervous conversation as she stopped the car along the kerb just down the block from the building where she lived. 'It's also considered something of a miracle. Are you coming?' she asked when Jason stared at her in stunned surprise.

He followed her along the pavement and then up the fourteen granite steps that led to her front door. A moment later they were in her small apartment. 'Do you want a cup of tea?' she asked, pretending to a casualness she didn't feel. 'I have herbal tea and Lipton's. Or coffee, if you'd prefer it.'

'Tea is fine,' he whispered, watching her as she slid off her coat. 'Whatever you're having.' Then he slid his hands into his pockets and glanced around the room, noting the comfortable, neat furnishings and the paintings on the walls.

They were going to make love, Andrea knew as she filled the tea kettle and set it on the burner. That was as inevitable as the rising of the sun, but neither one of them was going to speak about it for fear of breaking the fragile cord that seemed to bind them together in a universe of silent understanding.

She set two tea cups on a tray and filled them with hot water as Jason slid the jacket from his shoulders and tossed it across the couch. Then he noticed a novel on her bookshelf and picked it up. It was *Farther Now From Home*, she realised as she set the tea cups on the coffee table and sat cross-legged on her plush green rug to sip the cinnamon-rose tea.

'How did my father kill himself?' Jason asked her curiously.

'He took sedatives.' She laid her chin against her bent up knees and studied his sad face. 'Then he read that book until his heart stopped beating. The doctor said there wasn't any pain.' Jason nodded with relief.

'I wish I had told him that I loved him,' he said regretfully as he sat down and sipped his herbal tea. 'Before it was too late.'

'I think he knew,' Andrea answered sympathetically. 'He said you always took his phone calls, even though you ended up fighting every time you spoke. People don't always need to hear the words to know the truth.'

'Do you need to hear them?' he asked, reaching out to touch his fingers to her chin. 'Look at me, Angel,' he demanded hoarsely, lifting her face into the light.

She had no choice but to meet his eyes, and once she met them, she was too mesmerised to glance away. She felt herself tumbling headlong into a vast abyss of yearning from which there was to be no escape this time. 'I'm in love with you, Andy.' Jason said the words so softly she wondered if he had really said them or she only wished so desperately to hear them that she had imagined it. 'I've been in love with you for years, but I've refused to see that. Ten years ago . . .' he whispered painfully as he knelt beside her and let his hand open out against her smooth, flushed cheek. 'It was an agony to pretend I didn't want you when I wanted you so much. I dreamed of going to you and taking you in my arms. I could imagine the softness of your mouth against my skin, and I used to wonder . . .' His hand moved back to softly stroke her tangled auburn hair as he blurted out the words of his confession. 'I used to wonder what your hair smelled like.'

Andrea was too surprised to speak, and when he coaxed her back against the rug she gave no protest, feeling herself lost to an old dream she had lived a thousand times before. But in her dreams it was she who had ached with a desire she had been too young to fully understand. She had never realised that he had been filled with the same desperate hungers, too.

'That day I found you asleep under the oak tree on the lawn,' Jason confessed as he stretched himself beside her, 'I knelt down beside you and I kissed your hair.'

'What did it smell like?' Andrea asked him breathlessly.

'It smelled like oak leaves warming in the sun,' he answered as his mouth caressed her throat. 'Like ferns and summer shadows. It smelled like being lost and not caring if I was ever found again,' he admitted as his mouth found hers and lingered for a touch that was just a heartbeat long.

She closed her eyes, imagining herself asleep on the sun-warmed grass covered by a canopy of leafy shadows. She had dreamed of him leaning down to kiss her, and had never known it was far more than a dream.

'But I cared about *your* being lost. I knew that I could hurt you, Andy.'

'No . . .' Her answer was a moan of pleasure as his hand swept up her side, exploring the curves of her lithe, responsive body. 'I wanted you, Jason. Even then.'

'How could a fifteen-year-old girl know what she wanted from a man?'

Maybe that was true, but she wasn't fifteen now. Lost to the seductive spell that Jason had woven around her aching senses, Andrea lifted her face to meet his lips more fully, inviting a deepening of the caresses that had fallen like summer mist against her thirsty mouth.

'Andy . . .' He moaned softly as her mouth widened to encompass the boundaries of his. 'Be careful, love,' he warned, pushing down against her shoulders in a feeble attempt to stop their slide into a deepening desire. But her arms had circled him too firmly and his own passion conspired against his wary self-restraint.

'Andy,' he moaned hoarsely as if his very soul had opened in the moment he relaxed against her, and left him helpless in the face of a caress that had been promised long before this moment. It was she who led at first, giving herself up to a primitive arousal as his arms closed around her. Then he, too, was lost.

He had always loved her, Andrea understood as she clung to his strong shoulders. This was the same emotion they had felt ten years before, although the face of it had changed. If he had seemed aloof then it was only that he was holding back to save her from a passion she wasn't old enough to know. Now he shared that passion like the gift it was and she thought only of returning it in more than equal measure.

Jason's mouth moved down to brush the upper swells of her firm breasts, and when she didn't stop him, his hand followed, loosening the buttons of her sweater and pushing the lacy fabric of her bra aside until there was no boundary between his exploring mouth and her soft trembling flesh.

Her fingers slid through his hair, holding him to her as his tongue traced the arc of the pink aureole that surrounded her sharp-peaked nipple. Her breath caught in her throat as he pressed himself against her, his maleness hard and insistent against her softer flesh.

They were going to make love, she knew, shivering with a strange excitement at his eager, possessive touch. She couldn't stop him now that her whole heart and soul screamed out to know him as a woman knows a man. She didn't want to stop him now that fate had brought him back to her willing arms. She closed her eyes to calm her too easily aroused desire as Jason slipped the sweater from her shoulders and tossed it carelessly aside.

'You're so beautiful,' he murmured, catching her hands to press them back against the rug. Then his mouth met hers again, his passion doubled and redoubled with every deepening kiss until Andrea was lost beyond the boundaries of common sense and fear. There was nothing in the world now except a desire that reverberated through her senses, driving her deeper and deeper into Jason's insistently commanding arms.

'No . . .' Jason moaned, his voice so low and hoarse that Andrea's eyes flew open in confusion. His breaths were fast and shallow, his face tense as he tightened his arms beside her to take his weight. 'My God,' he asked in horror, 'what are we doing?'

'What are we doing?' she echoed weakly, feeling cold now that his arms had been withdrawn. She was still half-lost to the desire that dulled her mind, but she was frightened by the sight of his pain-racked face. She reached up to circle his shoulders and invite him back to the arms that ached to hold him, but Jason pulled away.

'Don't!' he warned her sharply. 'Don't touch me, Andy. Please!' He retrieved her sweater from the floor and tossed it on her lap. 'Put this back on,' he ordered, running his hand through his tangled mane of hair. 'Let's pretend that never happened.'

'I don't understand.' Andrea pushed herself up and hurriedly slipped the sweater on. One moment his embrace had been passionately intense. Now he stared fixedly out of the window to the street below as if he couldn't bring himself to look at her at all. What had she done to break the spell that had bound them both together in a moment of sheer ecstasy?

'I've known a lot of women,' he admitted in a throaty whisper as he let the curtain fall away from his tense hand. 'But none of them has ever scared me the way you do. You were going to let me make love to you, weren't you? Right here,' he gestured to the floor, 'right now, before we had a chance to think of anything but passion?'

'Yes,' she admitted in a breathy whisper.

'Then what?' he demanded. ' "Thank you, sir," and back to Robert?'

'I don't know what.' She hugged her trembling shoulders to ward off the misery she felt. 'I wasn't thinking about the future.'

'Well, maybe we both ought to think about it,' he answered cynically. 'Because I'm not too thrilled by the idea of being in love with my brother's wife.'

Did he still think she was going to marry Robert? Now? After she had fallen in love with him? 'I want *you*,' she protested. 'Not your brother.'

'When morning comes, you'll want my brother,' he predicted cynically. 'You'll have eighty-three million reasons to want Robert Dorning.' She stared at him with desperation, trying to unravel all the tangled emotions in her heart. She didn't care about the money. She wanted only Jason Dorning and his love, but she didn't know how to convince him of that fact.

'Look,' he said as he took his sheepskin jacket from the couch. 'All those things I said about kissing you while you slept, and the smell of your hair—That was all nonsense. I know what a woman wants to hear, so I said it. I was trying to seduce you, and now I've changed my mind.'

'I don't believe you,' Andrea answered firmly. Ten years ago he had refrained from hurting her. Now he was running away from desire because he didn't want to hurt himself. 'I think you love me.'

'I was lying,' Jason answered tersely. 'I'm not the man you want.'

'Jason? Wait!'

It was too late. He strode away and slammed the door behind him.

CHAPTER EIGHT

'PATIENCE is a virtue, Possess it if you can, Seldom found in woman, Never found in man . . .' Odd that she should think of that old rhyme right now, Andrea thought, clicking her fingernails impatiently against the cover of the phone book as she waited. Robert's secretary had put her call on hold.

'Andrea?'

She came to attention when she heard Robert's clipped, impatient voice. 'Robert,' she answered with relief. 'I thought I'd been forgotten. When I phoned in sick this morning, my office said that you had called.'

'Do you need a doctor?' he asked with quick concern.

'No! No, I don't,' she answered wearily, running her fingers through her tangled auburn curls. 'I had insomnia last night, that's all.' Funny what love could do to a hale and hearty woman, Andrea thought with a flash of cynical self-mockery. She had been awake all night, trying to decide what she should do. Nothing in her life was as clear as the certainty that she loved Jason Dorning, and that she would gladly give up everything to be with him. But she couldn't find the man. He hadn't told her where he was staying, and after calling thirty hotels and boarding houses it had occurred to her that he might

115

not be staying in a hotel at all. Jason had a lot of friends.

'I thought we could get together later today,' Robert suggested. 'You wanted to talk, didn't you?'

'Did your detective tell you anything?' Andrea asked, feeling her stomach knot with a sickening, apprehensive pain.

'These things take time . . .'

He hadn't found a thing, she realised, feeling foolish for her sudden doubts. Her heart told her everything she needed to know about the man she loved. She didn't need a private detective to tell her that he was an honest, decent man. 'That doesn't mean that there isn't something to find,' Robert added hastily. 'I just want a chance to talk to you before Jason does something else to undermine our engagement. Will you come to my office this afternoon? Say, three o'clock?' he asked.

'Yes,' Andrea agreed, sighing with relief. They'd talk it out, and then the engagement would be over. 'I'll see you then. Goodbye, Robert.' Their engagement had been a mistake from the beginning, she realised now. She had drifted into a relationship with Robert because she cared about him, but there had never been a spark of passion. If it hadn't been for Creighton Dorning's will, Robert probably never would have asked her to marry him at all, and she would have been free to go to Jason.

If she could have found Jason, she thought desperately, opening the phone book on her lap. If he had left Boston she might never find him. He could be in France or South America or . . . Green

Harbor, Maine! That was where he lived! she remembered now, flipping to the front of the phone book to find the number for information.

He wasn't there, either, Andrea realised, listening to the phone ring insistently at the other end of the long line. It was then she thought of Marla Winters and flipped through the phone book for the number of the State Street Theater. But before she had picked up the phone again, there was a knock on her apartment door.

'Andy?' a familiar voice called out.

'Jason?' She unlocked the door with trembling fingers and stared with relief at the man who stood there. His face was pale from lack of sleep and there were shadows under his dark eyes, but it didn't matter. He looked so wonderful to her she couldn't take her eyes off his exhausted face.

'I went by your office but they said that you were off sick today,' Jason said, letting his eyes move down from her hastily brushed curls to her weary face. 'Maybe you've got the same disease that I've got.'

'It's a possibility,' she agreed, stepping back to gesture him into her apartment. 'Do you suppose there's a cure?'

'No. I think it might be fatal.' He gave her a sheepishly weak smile, then he glanced restlessly away, as if he were embarrassed by his own emotions. 'I walked around the city most of the night,' he admitted. 'I even composed a rather nice speech. I don't suppose you want to hear it?'

'Sure.' Andrea leaned back against the door,

watching him curiously as he paced the room with nervous, restless strides.

'All right . . .' Jason took a breath to calm his shaky nerves. 'When this started all I wanted was to get you into my bed and out of my system. I didn't care what kind of lies I had to tell you.'

'And the things you said to me last night?' Andrea prompted. 'Were they lies, too?'

'No,' he admitted painfully. 'Last night I was lying to myself. I told myself that I was leaving because I didn't want to hurt you by ruining your engagement to my brother. But I left because I didn't want what you were willing to give me. I don't want an affair with my brother's fiancée, Andy,' he said bluntly. 'For the first time in my life a brief fling with a pretty woman isn't enough to make me happy. What I do want is . . . well . . .' he ran his fingers through his tousled hair to smooth it back from his forehead in a nervous gesture. 'It's going to sound a little crazy to you. I want someone to belong to. Children . . .'

Children? Andrea stared at him with incredulous amazement. Was Jason Dorning about to propose marriage to her?

'I want swing sets and bicycles in the front yard and runny noses,' he admitted wryly. 'The whole package that comes with them. A wife . . .'

'Children?' she echoed, leaning back against the door with a delighted smile. This *was* a proposal. It was not at all what she expected from a man who could be effusively poetic in his teasing conversations, but he wasn't teasing now. He was exhausted from the same kind of restless night she had spent, and he was being painfully, sincerely honest.

'I can give you a decent life,' he continued haltingly. 'I can't give you the kinds of things that Robert can afford, but if it's love you want...'

'I was hoping for a little lust,' Andrea interrupted his rambling proposal. 'You *do* feel lust, don't you?'

'Oh, yes,' he admitted, meeting her eyes with such a clarity of feeling that her lips stretched outward into a widening grin. 'I do feel that.'

'Then I suppose I should have your children,' she answered teasingly. 'Though I would prefer they come without the runny noses.'

'You're going to marry me?' he asked incredulously. 'Just like that?'

'Mm-hm.'

'What about the money? You'd be throwing away eighty-three million dollars. You know that, don't you?'

'I know what I'm doing,' Andrea answered evenly, touched by his reservations. 'I love you, Jason,' she assured him as she reached up to touch his cheek. 'And, rich or poor, I'll always love you. I just wish...' she met his dark-eyed stare with a flirtatious smile, '... that your proposal had been a little more romantic!'

'Romance? Is that what you want, love?' He grinned as his arms circled her slim waist. 'I adore you,' he said earnestly. 'You are the sun that rises in my morning sky. You are my violet-eyed gypsy, my beating heart, my soul ... My life!' he added enthusiastically as he lifted her from her feet and spun her around in a dizzy circle. 'You don't care about the money! You're going to marry me!'

'Yes!' Andrea agreed with giddy pleasure. She wrapped her arms around him until there were no boundaries between them. He didn't know that he would inherit half of the estate if she didn't marry Robert, and she decided to wait to tell him rather than spoil the romantic exuberance of the present moment. She'd keep that as a surprise for later, she decided, smiling as his lips softly touched her more than willing mouth.

'I can be a poor man's wife,' she reassured him when their lips had parted. 'I can even be a crazy man's wife. But an unfaithful man's wife is another matter.'

'Ah.' His grin was back, warm and mischievously attractive. 'I'll have to grow up now, won't I? All right,' he agreed. 'I'll tell you a secret. My sexual adventures have been greatly exaggerated.'

'You're really a virgin?' she guessed sarcastically.

'Well, no, they haven't been *that* exaggerated,' he said as picked her up and laid her on the couch. 'I'll bet this blouse is hot,' he suggested, unbuttoning it and pushing it back far enough to kiss the creamy skin along her throat. 'This bra looks hot, too. Better take it off before you get overheated.' His eyes were impishly amused as he slid his hands behind her and fumbled with the hooks of her lacy bra.

'My underclothes are not too hot!' she laughed, wriggling away from his impetuous embrace and glancing at the clock. It read two-thirty, and Robert expected her at three. 'I have to go now, Jason.'

'Go?' His face was comically dismayed. 'Is that your idea of romance? "I'll marry you. Goodbye."? Come here, cupcake. I've got something to teach you about men.' He made a move in her direction, but she eluded his quick hands.

'I have to go,' she repeated with more reluctance as she met his warm, brown eyes. 'But I'll be back later and then we'll make wedding plans.'

'We could fly to Las Vegas and be married tonight,' Jason suggested. 'I can't wait much longer for you, angel. It's been ten long years already.'

And it had been an eternity for her as well. Now that she knew how much he loved her, she ached to be inside the circle of his arms, possessing him and being possessed with equal urgency and fervour. She forced herself to look away lest her hunger rise so forcefully she wouldn't have the strength to leave.

'We could apply for a marriage licence here in Boston,' Jason suggested slowly, noting the pink flush that suffused her face. 'That would give me three days to respect your chastity and prove myself good enough for you—sort of like Ivanhoe.'

'What if I don't want my chastity respected?' Andrea laughed. 'Has that occured to you, my idiotic knight?'

'If you want me badly enough, I won't refuse you. I understand basic human needs.' His eyes were sparkling with mischievous humour as he strode across the room to catch her up in his strong arms. 'Why don't I go along to your appointment with you? You're finally getting that tattoo, aren't you?'

'No, I have to see . . . You're not going to like this,' she warned, touching his shoulders gently as if that one gesture could prevent his too-quick temper from exploding. 'I have to see Robert.'

'What?'

'Don't get upset about it,' she cajoled him. 'I have to tell him about us, because he deserves that much consideration. Technically, I'm *his* fiancée, but I'm going to run off and elope with you. I've got to give him some kind of explanation, don't I?'

'Sure,' Jason agreed curtly. 'Later. Elope with me tonight, then call him from Las Vegas. Better yet, *I'll* call him from Las Vegas.'

There was so much fear in his eyes that Andrea framed his face with her two hands and kissed his mouth with a soft reassurance. 'I don't love him the way I love you, Jason.'

'You love him some other way?' Jason demanded peevishly. 'I don't like this conversation, Andy. This isn't fun to listen to.'

'You're being unreasonable,' she argued.

'No, I'm not being unreasonable.' He broke away from her hands. 'I'm being terrified. Robert's going to find a way to stop us.'

'He can't do that.'

'Wake up and look around you!' Jason cried. 'We are some kind of miracle, and Robert's going to take that miracle away. He's not going to lose you to a man like me!'

'What can he say?' she attempted to humour him. 'That you're poor and crazy? I already know that, and I still love you.'

'You won't,' he predicted, meeting her eyes with so much fear her heart twisted with dark foreboding despite her own certainty of love.

'I *will*,' she insisted just as fiercely, meeting his mouth with one last reassuring kiss. 'You'll have to trust me Jason. I'll be back in just a little while. Then we'll fly to Las Vegas and be married.'

It was one matter to reassure Jason, and quite another matter to reassure herself, Andrea realised when she walked into Robert's office twenty minutes later. Robert looked far too smugly self-assured for a man who was about to lose half of an eighty-three-million-dollar legacy.

Vincent Carpezzi sat, troubled and uneasy, in a chair beside the window. He looked up only long enough to give her a weakly sympathetic smile.

They know something unpleasant about Jason, was Andrea's first thought, then she pushed her suspicions aside with a defensive stubbornness and faced Robert with all the dignity that she could muster. 'I think you already know what I came here to tell you, Robert. I never meant to fall in love with someone else, but now that I have I can't . . .'

'Sit down, Andrea,' Robert interrupted before she could go on. 'I have something you should hear first.'

She couldn't stop the trembling in her knees, but she retained her stubbornly brave smile. 'Did your detective find something?' she asked, deciding to face the situation squarely. 'You said he didn't.'

'My detective didn't. Not yet.' Robert faltered

only briefly. 'An investigation takes time. A week. Maybe as much as a month if he's used aliases and . . .'

'There's nothing.' She said it with complete assurance.

'Are you planning to marry him?' Robert demanded. Andrea nodded. 'Immediately?' She nodded once again.

Robert's eyes were dark and chilling, and his face registered a grim impatience as he sat down behind his desk. 'What kind of insanities did he tell you to make you willing to go away with a man you barely know?'

'He told me . . . things,' she muttered with stubborn loyalty. That she was more beautiful and desirable than any other woman he had known. That he loved her with his whole heart and soul. Those were the insanities that every woman longed to hear, and she was no different from the rest.

'I don't suppose he told you about my father's will?'

'The will?' Andrea was bewildered. She had been there when they saw the videotape. What else was there to know? 'If I don't marry you, the estate will be split equally between the two of you, but Jason doesn't even know that.'

'I'm afraid he may know more than you do.' Vincent Carpezzi spoke for the first time, staring at the carpet as if he were embarrassed by the delicacy of the proceedings in which he was forced to play a role. 'I didn't realise anything was amiss when Mr Dorning came to me—that's Mr Jason Dorning,' he elaborated to avoid confusion. 'He asked if he could have a copy of the taped will. For personal reasons, he explained it.'

'The most personal of reasons,' Robert interjected cynically. 'Greed.'

'Yes, well . . .' Vincent Carpezzi cleared his throat. 'Then you asked me what would happen if you didn't marry Robert. And I couldn't help noticing what went on at the Pantonnes' party, so I went back to my office and viewed the tape again. That's when I noticed the problem. I took the liberty of having a transcript made, which I have already shown Mr Dorning—Robert, I mean. I regret I didn't see the problem before Creighton Dorning's death, but it all seemed so straightforward then. I never imagined that it could be turned around another way.'

Andrea stared at the lawyer in confusion. Creighton Dorning had been absolutely clear: Robert was to inherit the estate upon their marriage.

'Here's the transcript,' Robert offered, handing her a sheaf of papers. 'I've underlined the paragraph that concerns us now.'

Andrea stared at the paper. *My son is to inherit my entire estate on the day that he marries Andrea McKinley. Until such time as the marriage takes place, Robert may continue as acting president of Dorning Imports.*

'Robert would have inherited the estate if we married,' Andrea said matter-of-factly. 'Now the

estate will be divided equally.' Vincent Carpezzi
was silent.

'Read it again, Andrea,' Robert commanded
evenly.

My son is to inherit . . . Andrea stared at the
paper, and suddenly she understood. Creighton
Dorning had two sons. The one who married her
would inherit everything.

'Do you think he knows?' she asked the lawyer,
feeeling her heart twist with a sickening pain. 'Do
you think that's why Jason said he loved me?' The
truth was clear enough in the old lawyer's eyes.

'Of course that's why he said it,' Robert answered
impatiently. 'Jason would do anything to take my
inheritance away. He hates me because I'm
everything he's not. But this . . . this . . .' he
spluttered, as if his brother had crossed a line he
couldn't imagine a man of any decency approach-
ing. 'To use a naïve woman so cruelly . . . To fill her
head with nonsense, and make a fool of her like
this . . .'

It wasn't true. It couldn't be. This was nothing
more than a ghastly misunderstanding, Andrea told
herself, staring numbly at the paper in her hand.
'Jason loves me,' she repeated firmly, willing the
words to be hard fact. 'He doesn't even know about
the money. I'll go to him and he'll tell me that he
doesn't know.'

'He'll tell you another pack of lies,' Robert
answered cynically. 'He's certainly not going to
admit that he's marrying you for the inheritance.
Though he might tell me,' he suggested, reaching

for the phone. 'No doubt he'd love to rub my face in his success. Where is he now?'

'He's at my apartment.'

Robert dialled the number, then flipped a button on the phone so that they all could hear the call.

'Hello?' It was Jason's voice that reverberated through the room. 'Andy?'

'Andrea left my office a few minutes ago,' Robert responded coolly. 'I've called to offer my congratulations. For your marriage and for the money you're about to come into. It seems that I badly underestimated your talents.'

There was a long moment of silence before Jason answered. 'You know about the money?' he asked warily.

'Yes. I know quite a bit about you, Jason,' Robert lied. 'To tell the truth, I've had you investigated.'

Jason knew about the will. The transcript trembled in Andrea's suddenly cold hand and her heart knotted with an anguished pain. His falteringly nervous proposal had been an act to make her think that he had been as surprised as she had been by the unexpected nature of their love.

'You bastard,' Jason gave a dry, unpleasant laugh, 'I suppose you told Andrea all of my grubby little secrets?'

'I tried, but she wouldn't listen.'

Everything had been an act, Andrea realised now. His passion and his reluctance to make love to his brother's fiancée had all been planned to seduce her into a marriage that would give him the Dorning estate. And he had played his part so brilliantly she had never guessed that he had been lying. He had never wanted her. He had wanted his father's money.

'I'll tell her everything myself,' Jason offered evenly. 'After we're married, of course.'

'Of course,' Robert smiled coldly as he cast a glance at Andrea's pale cheeks. 'There's no sense in telling the goose too much before you get your hands on the golden egg.'

'What in hell does that mean?'

'Nothing,' Robert answered. 'I was just talking to myself. Goodbye, Jason.' He hung up the phone with a firm thud.

Everything had been a lie, she knew as she crumpled the transcript in her hand. Jason had never cared about her, but he understood women well enough to know which lies thay wanted most to hear.

'Do you see why I had to stop you?' Robert asked her evenly.

'Yes.' The word emerged mechanically from a vast cave of emptiness inside her. To lose Jason's love was hard enough, but with it she lost herself as well. All that was soft and womanly about her seemed to be slipping from her grasp. All the laughter and excitement were receding from her mind like an aching echo that grew weaker with every second's dim reverberation until she was what she had been before Jason Dorning had swept through her life: a calm and competent woman who would grow old watching others feel the passions that were denied to her.

'I have half a mind to have him arrested. Damn the scandal!' snapped Robert, infuriated. 'Let people talk. I want my brother locked up for this!'

'Hmph . . .' Vincent Carpezzi cleared his throat as if he were asking for permission to speak his mind. 'Technically speaking, there is no crime, so I don't think your interests would be served by . . .'

'No crime?' Robert exploded. 'What do you call seducing a woman for money? Do you call that integrity?'

'No,' the lawyer agreed reluctantly, casting a sympathetic glance at Andrea's pale face and empty, hopeless eyes. 'But it's not a criminal offence, either. Nor is it a misdemeanour, though some people would feel strongly that . . .'

'Nothing happened between us.' Nothing except falling headlong into the kind of love she had only dreamed about before. Her mistake had been believing her life was a romance, when it was actually a dark comedy of revenge and greed.

Both men stared at her, and on both faces there was a marked relief. It was the lawyer who recovered first. 'No, of course not,' he agreed quite happily. 'No one would ever suggest that, I'm sure . . . A woman of your character, after all . . .'

Andrea smiled wearily, wondering how it was possible for others to know so little about Andrea McKinley. Caught up in the throes of a passionate hunger for Jason's arms, she would have given him ten times over what he asked. It was only a quirk of fate that she hadn't had the time to make a greater fool of herself than she already was.

'There were a few kisses, that was all.' She met
Vincent Carpezzi's eyes, surprised by a wisdom
there that seemed as old as time, rubbed thin by too
much life. There were kisses, and they were
everything to her. That understanding was reflected
in the gaze they shared for one short, silent moment.
Then, with the reflex of a gentleman who has seen a
private torment and has chosen not to add
embarrassment as well, the man glanced restlessly
away.

'I ... er ...' he rose from his chair beside the
window, 'I should be going now.' He held out his
hand to Robert. 'I trust that the rest of your
conversation will be personal, not legal.'

Whether that was an opinion or a suggestion,
Andrea didn't know, but he said nothing more to
Robert Dorning. 'Goodbye, Miss McKinley.' He
held out his hand, and when she met it he surprised
her by lifting her hand to his lips. 'If I were younger,
my dear, I would suggest another suitor for your
hand.'

'Thank you, Mr Carpezzi,' she whispered weakly, grateful for his unexpected chivalry.

A moment later the lawyer closed the door
behind him, and Andrea faced Robert all alone. She
expected a lecture about her foolishness, but he
surprised her, too. 'The past few weeks have been
difficult for all of us,' he suggested as he approached
her chair and let his hand rest tentatively against
the arching back. 'I know how much you must have
wanted comfort after my father's death, and I was
too blind to think of anything but the business.'

That wasn't entirely the truth, Andrea knew, gritting her teeth together to stop the cry that gathered in her throat. Her attraction to Jason was too primitive and elemental to be explained away as a need for comfort after Creighton Dorning's death.

'Andrea . . .' Robert's hand fell hesitantly to her trembling shoulder and then withdrew as she burst into sobs. 'I'm sorry,' he muttered feebly. 'Don't cry, Andrea. I don't know what to do.' He fumbled in his pocket and withdrew a linen handkerchief which he tendered hopefully.

'Thank you.' She pressed the cloth against her face and took a breath to calm her crushing sense of anguish. 'I'm the worst kind of a fool,' she confessed in halting, gulping words. 'I'm the kind of woman who believes flattery even when she knows it can't be true.'

'No.' Robert stopped her, laying his hand imploringly against her arm in a touch that was more sympathetic than she had any right to expect. 'My father said I shouldn't take you for granted, but I didn't listen. You were always there for me, Andrea. You were so patient and understanding that I grew selfish.'

'It wasn't your fault.'

'It *was*,' he insisted. 'If I had told you all those things you wanted to hear you wouldn't have listened to Jason. I know that now. Thank God it's not too late to save what we once had.'

It *was* too late, she knew, adding guilt to her already overwhelming grief. Jason had hurt her by pretending love, and now she would hurt his brother by refusing to do just that. Not returning love in equal measure was a sword whose blade was razor-sharp and cruel no matter how gently it was wielded.

'I don't talk about my feelings easily,' Robert confessed, sinking to his knees beside her chair and covering her hand with his. 'But that doesn't mean I don't have them.'

'Don't . . .' cried Andrea. 'Please get up, Robert,' she implored, hoping he wouldn't blurt out too much and end up hating her when it was over.

'I love you, Andrea.'

'Oh, God, don't . . .'

'I'm no less a man than he is.' Robert pressed his face against her lap as if he were petitioning forgiveness. 'I can't use words the way he does, but I'm no less a man.'

'I know,' she admitted painfully, laying her hand against his thick brown hair and letting her fingers curve against it. 'I wish I didn't have to hurt you.'

He was silent for so long she thought that there was nothing more to say, but finally he stirred and looked up to meet her eyes with a pleading earnestness that tore her heart in two. 'Marry me, Andrea,' he whispered desperately. 'Marry the man who loves you, and I'll try to be the man you want.'

He couldn't be, she knew. He was no more like Jason than the moon was like the dazzling, exploding sun. But he was decent and good. Perhaps in time she could grow to love him with an affectionate constancy that would outlast the bursting fireworks of passion.

She touched his cheek and let her hand fan out against it in a tender, soothing touch. 'I can't marry you, Robert. Not now. I need time to find out who I am before I try to be someone else's wife.'

He didn't disagree, although his pain showed clearly in his eyes. 'All right,' he whispered finally. 'I'll give you time, if that's what you want.'

He laid his head against her lap again in a gesture of weary resignation and Andrea softly stroked his cheek, feeling a kinship with the man now that they were both the victims of a love they couldn't have. She could try to make him a good wife, but when she went to his bed she knew she would dream of Jason's touch. How long could any man live with that kind of emotional betrayal before he started hating his own wife?

At length Robert lifted his head and sat back on his heels, giving her a weakly optimistic smile. 'We still have reservations at the Hermitage. Let me finish,' he cautioned when she opened her mouth to object. 'We could go as friends, Andrea. I won't ask for more than you can give me. I just thought it would be good for you to get away. It would give you time to think about what you want from life.'

What a dear, sweet man he was, Andrea thought, nodding her agreement. It would do her a world of good to leave the greyness of the city behind her for a while. Maybe a change of scenery would help to drive the images of Jason out of her tortured heart and remind her of the level-headed woman that Andrea McKinley once had been.

CHAPTER NINE

ANDREA touched the tissue-wrapped red roses she had found on the seat of the chauffeured limousine, surprised by Robert's gesture. It had been uncharacteristically impractical for him to send flowers on the day they were leaving for Virginia, but in the past week Robert had been both impractical and touchingly attentive.

He had arranged her leave of absence from work, and he had insisted on being the one to contact Jason with the message that Andrea had changed her mind and didn't want to see him. He had even arranged to have her stay in a hotel under an assumed name so Jason couldn't find her. He had lifted every burden that he could from her fragile shoulders, but still he couldn't lift the burden of her loving the wrong man.

Robert was good and kind and honest, but her appreciation of those virtues had nothing at all to do with the kind of passion a woman should feel before she went to a man's arms. If she married him she would be cheating him, and she had too much integrity for that.

Andrea leaned back against the plush upholstery of the car and tried to concentrate on the Christmas lights as the car crawled through the evening traffic in the city. But all she could think about was Jason with his quicksilver grin and generous, warm laugh. He had betrayed her in the cruellest way by pretending to a love he didn't feel, she reminded herself ruthlessly, forcing his image out of her imagination.

It wasn't six o' clock yet, but the winter twilight brought a violet-grey duskiness to the city streets, and the yellow street lamps glowed like angels' haloes in the icy air. 'I love you, angel . . .' Andrea could hear the inflection of Jason's masculine, low voice. He had been lying to her. All he wanted was the money he would inherit if she married him. He had confessed to that himself.

And yet, there had been moments when she had been transformed under Jason's soft, approving gaze. She had believed she was his angel, if only for the fleeting moment in which he had woven his spell around her to keep reality at bay. Now that veil of illusion had fallen into tatters and reality pressed in like an icy wind she had to steel herself against.

'Mr Dorning says he's sorry.'

'What?' Andrea struggled to push back her unhappy thoughts.

'He says he's sorry,' the driver repeated as he manoeuvred the car on to the entrance road to Logan Airport. 'He can't fly down with you tonight because something came up at the office, but he'll have someone meet you in Virginia to take you to the Hermitage Hotel. He'll be there by morning.'

'Oh.' She was hardly surprised. Despite Robert's

romantic gestures the past week, he was a businessman. If there was a crisis at the office, he would
attend to it before he left for Christmas vacation in
another state. The chauffeur bypassed the crowded
terminals in favour of a smaller, chartered airline.

'Wing and a Prayer Airlines,' the pilot joked,
loading her baggage into the waiting plane.
'Dorning says you're not the timid type.'

'If you're not afraid of crashing, neither am I,'
Andrea answered as she buckled herself into one of
the seats in the small cabin. It had been meant as a
joke, but there was far too much truth in her
rejoinder. Right now she had frighteningly little
interest in whether she lived or died.

As if he sensed that fatalism, and found it
confusing, the pilot fell silent as he made the final
checks. 'All set,' he informed her as he came
through the cabin again. 'It may take us a while to
get clearance from the tower, but when we do, we'll
go.'

'Thank you.' Andrea smiled distractedly, relieved when he disappeared through the cockpit
door and left her in solitary silence. She closed her
eyes and tried in vain to fight back her memories of
Jason.

Despite the pilot's joke, it was an uneventful
flight. Andrea looked out occasionally to see the
thin ribbons of light that cut the dark terrain into
squares of city blocks and tentacles of highway, but
the lights that might have warmed the inhabitants
below served only to make her feel as cold and lost
as a voyager among the stars.

At last she felt the loss of altitude and looked out of the window at the small airport below, surprised by the white covering of snow that glistened coldly under the wintry, silver moonlight. There had been no snow in Boston, and it was odd that she should fly south to find it.

'Signed, sealed, and delivered, all before the blizzard hits,' the pilot declared cheerfully as he came back through the cabin to open up the door.

'There's going to be a blizzard?' Andrea asked dully as she stepped out into the sharp December air. The moon sailed high and silver, but already there was a gauzy covering of clouds that floated across it like a fluttering, slow-moving veil. A jeep chugged up along the runway, but she barely noticed the dark-jacketed figure who got out and ambled towards the plane. The man was from the hotel, she guessed, as she watched the two men load her luggage into the jeep.

Jason loved the snow. He loved the brooding silence before it came and then the release of tension as the white cascading feathers swirled to the ground below. He liked the smell of pine trees on a hot August day, and the first shy crocuses that poked out of the ground in spring. It was odd that she knew that much about Jason Dorning, but didn't know what Robert thought of snow.

Andrea didn't wait to hear what conversation transpired between the men. She walked to the jeep and opened the passenger door to climb in, staring out of the window at a landscape that reminded her of Jason. *Everything* reminded her of Jason, she realised unhappily. He had insinuated himself into her life so completely that he was as much a part of her as the air she breathed.

She heard the door thud shut and noted the man beside her as he turned the key in the ignition. He wore a broad brimmed hat that made him seem like an adventurer bent on shady dealings, but Andrea supposed her sudden chill of apprehension was only a figment of a tortured imagination whose boundaries were now beyond her absolute control. He was a hired man from the Hermitage Hotel, no more, no less, and her premonitions of danger would dissolve if she stopped focusing on her melancholy grief for a man whose love she had never truly had.

'I didn't expect Virginia to be so cold,' she said conversationally. The man's only answer was a grunt that might have been assent as the jeep turned on to a secondary highway and began to pick up speed.

'Does it snow here often?' Andrea tried again, only to be rewarded with an evasive mutter. She studied him with frank alarm. The brim of his hat hid his shadowed face, but there was something far too familiar about the tension in his posture. When she realised what it was she looked again at the snowy landscape and the pine trees that lined the almost deserted road, comprehending everything in a shattering moment of illumination that left her too breathlessly stunned to speak.

They weren't in Virginia. She didn't know where they were, but she knew who sat beside her in the jeep. 'Jason?' she whispered weakly. He glanced in her direction just long enough to confirm her fears. It was Jason Dorning who had met the plane. *His* plane, she understood, trying to unravel the series of events that had brought her to him so naïvely unaware. His plane, his driver. They hadn't even lied to her, she realised, sucking in a breath to calm her shaking nerves. She had walked into the trap as innocently as a lamb, her mind too numb with grief to care where she was being taken.

'You're kidnapping me,' she said, stunned by the boldness of his action, and the risks that he was taking. Robert would go to the police, and they would know who had taken her. 'Take me back now, and nothing will happen to you, Jason,' she pleaded. 'I don't want you to do something you'll regret.'

His fingers tightened around the steering wheel. 'You know I won't hurt you.' His words were an angry accusation, a reminder that she hadn't gone back to talk to him after she had seen Robert, but she sensed the honesty behind his harshly muttered fury. The danger she was facing wasn't physical. The danger lay in being forced to be with a man she loved more than reason.

'Good of you to come around and explain things,' Jason suggested bitterly. 'But maybe you don't feel you have to explain anything to the bastard member of the family.'

'It wasn't that . . .' Andrea muttered miserably. She had been afraid to see him for fear she would believe another pack of lies. 'Robert said he called you.'

'Oh, he did.' Jason's jaw tensed when he answered. 'My fiancée's fiancé called to tell me that you were going to marry him after all, and that you didn't want me to contact you again. He threw in a few choice legal terms ... "harassment" ... "restraining order" ... Little goodies like that.'

'I'm sorry,' Andrea apologised. 'I should have told you myself, but I was too much of a coward.' He cast her a sidelong, angry glance, but he didn't answer.

They drove for an hour in sullen silence while the darkness closed around them like a cloak and the first clotted flakes of snow drifted down across the windscreen. Then Jason slowed and turned abruptly, following a rutted dirt road as it plunged more deeply into the darkness of the pines. Andrea held tightly to the door frame as they bounced and jolted forward.

The claustrophobically dark woods finally opened to reveal a field and a house set dramatically against a cliff. Jason pulled the jeep into the garage and snapped the key to kill the engine. 'I'll get your bags,' he offered.

'I'm not getting out of this jeep until you drive me back to the airport,' Andrea announced decisively. 'I'd have to be a fool to go along with this insanity!'

Jason didn't argue. 'Suit yourself,' he muttered. A moment later he had carried her suitcases through a door and shut it behind him, leaving her stubbornly defiant and shivering from the cold.

She hated him, she decided, livid with fury now. He had swept into her neatly ordered life as if he owned her. He had lied and humiliated her, and then he left her here alone. She would freeze to death before she went inside, she promised herself stubbornly, changing her mind fifteen minutes later when the wind picked up and howled like a banshee through the shaking trees.

He had won the first round, she conceded, slipping off her coat and dropping it across a kitchen chair. The air was redolent with spices from whatever bubbled in the cast iron kettle on the stove and Jason presided over it like a sorcerer concocting a magic potion. He stopped only long enough to lift a screeching teapot off a burner and pour two cups of tea.

Andrea didn't break their silence. Instead, she moved past him to enter the next room. It was an enormous living room with a cathedral ceiling and a large fireplace made of granite blocks, but it was the windows that commanded her attention. One entire wall was glass.

'In the morning you'll be able to see the ocean.' Jason placed a cup of tea on the low pine coffee table and came across the room. She moved away, but he didn't follow. Instead he flicked a switch and a floodlight outside cast a burst of illumination across the swirling snow. 'There's a beach at the foot of the cliff,' he volunteered. 'You can see it from the terrace.'

Was he trying to impress her with someone else's house? She levelled a cool gaze in his direction. 'Are you the winter caretaker here?'

He met her eyes for a long moment in which

anger seemed to mix with disappointment. 'I must
be,' he answered cynically. 'A man like me couldn't
build a house like this, could he?'

'I didn't mean that.' She crossed her arms in front
of her as if they were a shield to ward off the desire
she felt too easily when he was near. She couldn't
afford to love him, not now that she knew what he
really wanted. Still, she wished he would take her in
his arms and prove with kisses what he could no
longer prove with words.

There was a pine tree in the corner of the room,
set firmly on a stand but as yet undecorated. He had
waited for her, she understood, feeling uneasy with
the scene of cosy domesticity he had created to win
her back. A Christmas tree and crackling logs on
the hearth, she thought, kneeling down beside the
fire to sip her herbal tea. The only flaw in the
Norman Rockwell setting was the kidnapping that
had brought her here.

'I bought the herbal tea for you,' Jason admitted
evenly, easing himself down beside her on the rug. 'I
tried to get the brand you made that night in your
apartment.' Andrea didn't answer.

'Would it be so hard to smile at me, Andy? That's
all I want, love,' he admitted in a whisper as he
leaned forward to catch her chin in his cupped
hand. 'Smile at me and give me hope.'

His thumb edged up to stroke her hot, flushed
cheek with so much devoted tenderness that she
could feel the floodgates of her common sense
straining before the weight of the desire he could
arouse too easily. His hand moved up to stroke her

auburn hair. 'You are so very beautiful, my darling.'

'Don't!' Her cry was sharp and filled with pain as she pulled away from his warm hands. 'Don't lie to me, Jason. I deserve better than that.'

'What am I lying about now, Andy?' he sighed wearily, closing his eyes to quiet his impatience.

'I'm not beautiful,' she said stubbornly.

'Fine,' he muttered angrily as he stood up and moved away. 'You're not beautiful. And I'm not in love with you. Is that what you want to hear?'

No, she thought morosely, hugging her arms to still their trembling under his impatiently dark eyes. She wanted to hear exactly what she couldn't let herself believe—that he loved a beautiful angel named Andrea McKinley.

Jason left the room without another word, returning a moment later with a tray which he set on the coffee table. 'It's venison stew. I didn't put drugs in your bowl, but if you think I did, we can trade.'

'I didn't say you did,' she answered sullenly, easing herself down to the rug to sit cross-legged beside the table.

'You have a hundred ways of saying I'm a no-good wastrel, lady.' His voice vibrated with a fierceness that frightened Andrea. 'I don't know why I expected better from you. Maybe I wanted it so much. I hoped . . .' His voice trailed off, and Jason pursed his mouth into an angry frown. 'Eat your stew,' he ordered tersely. 'I made it for you.'

Andrea took the bowl from the table and tried it, surprised by the delicious taste. 'It's good,' she admitted honestly, trying to build one small bridge back from the sullen fury that darkened Jason's handsome face. 'I'm surprised you can cook. That a man cooks so well,' she added hastily, noting the renewed anger that sparked to life in his eyes. 'Most of the men I know can't boil an egg.'

'Robert has never had to.'

'That's true,' she acknowledged, studying him with open curiosity. He had wilfully turned his back on the life his father had offered him, but in doing that he had faced another life. She only knew bits and pieces of the pleasures he had found there: the sweep of snow on a velvety dark night, the smell of pine trees in the sun, the warmth of willing arms and mouths.

At that thought she looked away, focusing her eyes on the restless, darting flames. He would have found no lack of willing women. He was an attractive man, and there was a sensual power in every move he made. She more than anyone understood the seductive nature of that dark, unpredictable masculinity that still held her in its thrall.

She ate her stew in silence, listening to the hissing of the steam that was driven from the burning logs and the echoing sweep of snow outside the window as it descended in an avalanche of swirling flakes. The only other sound was the sharp clicking of a clock above the mantel, separating each minute of uneasy silence from the one that came before.

'I'll do the dishes,' Andrea offered as she set her empty bowl down on the tray.

'Don't worry about them,' answered Jason. 'The maid will do them later.'

'You have a maid?'

'It was a joke.' His mouth curved upward slightly at the corners as if he were amused by her gullibility, and the eyes that met hers had returned to a more good-natured light.

'Oh.' She returned his smile so automatically she barely knew she'd done it until that smile was reflected in his own softening eyes. Then he reached out to touch her, his hand stopping in the air between them as if he had encountered a solid wall of glass when she stepped backward with a nervous motion.

Jason withdrew his hand and glanced around the high-ceilinged room with restless indecision. 'I waited for you before I decorated the tree,' he said, forcing his voice to a lighter, conversational tone, although the eyes that wouldn't gaze in her direction still seemed tortured by a desire he forced into restraint.

Did he really love her? Andrea wondered, barely able to hold back a wave of hope that threatened to extinguish common sense for ever. Or was it a transient desire, lust grown stronger by the very fact of having it denied?

Jason stood up abruptly and strode towards the tree, pulling out a box of decorations. 'I don't have a lot of them because I've never had a Christmas tree before. But I thought I would this year.'

Andrea followed him reluctantly. Anything was better than sitting before the fire in an uneasy

silence that stretched time to an unbearable
eternity. But she didn't miss the danger of the
domestic scene he had created to win her naïve
trust. As the storm closed in around them and the
fire flickered shafts of light across the cream-
coloured walls, she was too aware of her own
vulnerability to sentiment and love.

She knelt on the plush, orange rug beside him and
opened the nearest box. It was filled with coils of
tiny fairy lights. Every light a lover's heart, she
remembered his romantic story about the crystal
lights that lit the maples on the Commons. He
would have thought of that when he chose the
decorations. She laid the coil of lights on her lap and
turned away to hide her misery from Jason's
watchful eyes, but he had seen it.

His hand fell softly against her shoulder and then
his fingers tightened to hold her there when she
tried to pull away. 'What went wrong, Andy?' he
asked so plaintively she felt her heart constrict. 'I
thought you loved me.'

'I found out about . . .' She stopped herself before
she said too much. Jason would counter every
accusation with another lie, and she was too
trusting to sift truth from lies where he was
concerned. '. . . myself,' she said instead. 'I was
attracted to you for a while, but Robert helped me
see the truth about myself.'

'That was good of him,' Jason snapped sarcastically. 'What truth did my brother help you see?
That if you marry him you'll be a wealthy woman?'

'No.' The touch of his hand against her shoulder

was an agony to endure, but she clenched her teeth
and took a breath before she answered. 'That I'm
not a gypsy queen or a witch. I'm just a woman who
loves a man.'

'Robert?' he demanded, his fingers tightening
even more until they pressed against her flesh with
cruel insistence. 'Are you going to tell me that you
love my brother?'

'Yes,' Andrea lied. Maybe it would be easier if he
thought she loved another man. But Jason reacted
to her answer with a burst of anger.

'Look at me when you say that, Andy!' He turned
her roughly in his arms, forcing her to meet the dark
impatience of his furious brown eyes. 'Do you love
my brother?'

'Yes!'

'And you're going to marry him?' he demanded,
pushing her back against the floor and holding her
shoulders down against the rug to still her panicked
struggles. 'Say it, Andy. Say, "I love your brother
enough to spend the rest of my life with him. In his
house. In his bed. In his arms." Say it!' he demanded, giving her shoulders an impatient shake.

She was too frightened by his fury to meet his
eyes, but she found the strength to answer. 'I'm
going to marry your brother.'

'And you're happy?' he goaded.

'Yes,' Andrea lied, close to tears now with his
inquisition. 'I'm very happy.'

'Then why . . .' Jason twined his fingers through
her auburn curls, holding her so fast she was forced
to meet his angry eyes at last. 'Why do you look like

six kinds of Hell, angel?' he demanded bluntly, examining her pale skin and shadow-ringed, unhappy eyes.

'You're a very poor liar, Andy,' he whispered in the sullen silence that followed his blunt questions. Then, before she could stop him, his mouth descended to touch hers, softly at first, and then with more insistence as she struggled to break free from the very embrace her heart cried out to know.

She fought him, and then she fought herself, struggling to remain aloof from the mind-numbing magic of his mouth as it opened over hers with firm entreaty. When he pressed himself against her, his lean male body commandingly seductive against her softer woman's flesh, she stirred with one last fear-filled defiance before Jason's embrace brought her to the brink of an anguished sacrifice to all the forces she could not control.

She was his, she understood as his hand moved up beneath her sweater, exploring and reassuring and branding her with his possession all with the same touch. It didn't matter that he lied or that he didn't love her. His touch could move her to the brink of passion where she existed only as a woman bound by his commanding spell.

'Don't cry, angel.' Jason's voice was soft and pleading as he bent down to kiss away the tears that etched her trembling cheeks. 'I don't want to hurt you.'

He pulled away enough to study her anguished face and then he touched his fingers to her cheek so softly it seemed like a feather lingered there instead.

'Why did you run away from me?' he asked her plaintively. 'Was it the money?'

'Yes.' Her answer came from deep inside her, from a tortured well of misery where she understood how much she loved a man who could use her for revenge.

'It mattered that much to you?' he whispered. 'I thought you weren't like other women.'

No, she wasn't any different than any other woman, except perhaps that she had been a bigger fool. She had wanted to believe he loved her, and she had been willing to ignore the truth.

'I thought you loved me,' she said painfully, staring at the ceiling to stop her growing tears. 'It hurt to know that you only wanted the estate. At least Robert loved me more than that.'

There was a long moment of silence in the room, and then it was broken by Jason's honestly bewildered voice. 'What, in God's name, are you talking about?'

'Don't you know?'

'No!'

Was he lying? Andrea met his eyes with exultant hope. 'If I marry you, you inherit everything.' She watched his face, but there was no change there. Confusion was the only emotion on his handsome features. 'You asked Mr Carpezzi for a copy of the tape so you could study it.'

'The tape?' Jason echoed. With that, he got up and strode away abruptly. Andrea followed him to the kitchen where he rummaged through a stack of items on the counter and finally found a tape. 'I have a VCR in my bedroom,' he announced. 'I want to see this revelation for myself.'

Andrea wasn't sure if that was an invitation to follow, but she did, running to catch up with his long-legged strides up a curving stairway to the second floor. She sat down on the edge of his large bed while Jason pushed the tape into a slot in his videotape machine and flicked on the TV set.

A second later Creighton Dorning was greeting them. 'It's later in the tape,' Andrea suggested. 'After he tells Robert he wants grandchildren.' Jason picked up the remote control and pressed the fast forward button, watching the image of his father flicker on the screen.

'. . . is to inherit my entire estate . . .' Jason backed it up. 'My son is to inherit my entire estate on the day that he marries Andrea McKinley.' He backed it up again, and squinted at the screen, listening to the words once more before understanding spread across his face.

'I'll be damned,' he whispered. 'I never saw that. Have *you* seen it yet, cupcake?' he asked so unexpectedly she met his eyes in blank bewilderment, wondering why he seemed so thoroughly amused.

'He set us up,' he informed her, pointing at the frozen image of his father on the screen. 'Who was his favourite author?'

'Joseph Dalton.'

'No, the other one.'

'Jarvis Drew, I suppose, but . . .'

'Right!' Jason said triumphantly. 'Whose books

were in that box my father left me?'

'Jarvis Drew's,' she admitted reluctantly. 'But that doesn't prove anything.'

'Which book was on top? I'll bet it was *Hand From the Grave*. God, I should have seen it!' Jason laughed delightedly. 'That old goat left me a message that was six yards wide, and I would have seen it if I hadn't been so busy watching you. What did he want, angel? Tell me what you think.'

'I think you're getting carried away,' Andrea cautioned. 'Your father made a mistake, and now you're . . .'

'He didn't make any mistakes, Andy,' Jason interrupted, pointing the remote control to rewind the film. 'This tape is a bloody work of art. Watch this.'

He stopped the tape, then pushed a button to bring the image back to life. 'He said he'd never take my money, and he didn't even want my name . . .' Jason stopped the tape and propelled it forward. '. . . To tell the God's honest truth, he doesn't even *know* what he has. I'm talking about Andrea . . . How long do you think it would have taken Jason to drag her off to bed?'

'Do you see what he wanted?' Jason asked, easing himself down beside her on the bed. 'He wanted Robert to stop taking you for granted, and he wanted me to have part of the estate, but he knew I wouldn't take it unless I thought I had taken it from Robert. He planned to get two birds with one stone. The one thing he didn't consider was that you might

marry me and leave Robert with absolutely nothing. A woman like you,' he grinned so broadly
Andrea wondered if he were going to burst into a
laugh. 'My God, it would have been inconceivable
to the old man, wouldn't it? He thought you had too
much common sense to marry a barbarian like me.'

'I suppose it could be true,' she reluctantly
admitted. It was the kind of convoluted situation
that would have appealed to Creighton Dorning.
He wanted his son Robert to appreciate Andrea
McKinley, and what better way to accomplish that
than to create a competition for her hand? If, in the
process, he could trick Jason into taking part of the
inheritance, so much the better. Andrea didn't
approve of the way he had gone about it, but she
had to admit that the scheme was logical. How
could Creighton have expected her to fall in love
with the wrong Dorning son?'

'It never occurred to him that I could end up with
everything,' Jason grinned, bending his arms back
behind his head to stare up at the ceiling. 'What a
wonderful stroke of irony this is! I'm going to marry
you and inherit eighty-three million dollars. And for
once in his blue-blooded life, Robert is going to
have absolutely nothing.'

Andrea looked at Jason with appalled distaste.
Did he really think she would go along with
disinheriting his brother? 'I'm not going to marry
you,' she answered firmly. 'Not if it means leaving
Robert with nothing. I love you,' she admitted. 'I'll
live with you. I'll even have your children, but I
won't disinherit Robert.'

'I'm not having bastards, Andy,' Jason warned her, reaching out to take a cigarette from a package on the bedside table.

'Then you'll have to figure out a way to marry me without leaving Robert in the cold.'

'He would have been happy enough to leave *me* in the cold,' Jason reminded her cynically as he lit the cigarette with his silver lighter. 'I don't see any need for you to be this loyal to a man who was going to marry you for the inheritance.'

'He loves me,' she disagreed. 'Maybe more than you do.'

'You know that isn't true.'

'Then prove it!' Andrea challenged, knowing that if she didn't bring some peace to the Dorning family there was no chance for happiness with Jason. No matter how much she loved Jason Dorning, she couldn't turn her back on Robert as if he had never mattered in her life. 'Talk to him,' she insisted, picking up the phone on his bedside table and dialling Robert's number. 'Tell him you want to settle this inheritance business once and for all.'

Jason hesitated for a moment, then he spoke into the phone. 'Hello? This is Robert Dorning's brother. I wonder if I could speak to him. Oh . . . I see . . . Thank you.'

'Well, you're going to get what you want,' he smiled weakly as he replaced the phone and glanced up at the window. 'He's on his way. If this storm lets up, he should be here by morning.'

CHAPTER TEN

'YOU'RE up early,' Andrea commented to the man who sat beside the window in the living room, watching the first moments of dawn transform the sky to a steely grey. She had slept restlessly herself, worried about Robert travelling in the storm, but Jason still wore the same jeans and sweater he had worn the night before and she guessed that he hadn't even tried to sleep. 'What did you do all night?' she asked.

'I was listening to the storm broadcasts on the radio,' he admitted. 'Robert's not foolish enough to keep driving if things get bad, is he?'

'I don't know,' she answered honestly, touched by his concern. Part of him might hate his brother and all the childhood hurts that Robert stood for, but they were brothers after all. They both had Dorning blood inside their veins, and Andrea suspected that meant more to Jason than he had been willing to admit before.

'The storm has finally let up,' she said, gazing out the window at the pristine whiteness that spread out around them. 'It's pretty, isn't it?'

'Hm,' Jason murmured distractedly. Then he stood up abruptly. 'I'm going out,' he anounced a moment later, returning from the hallway with his ski parka, which he slid across his shoulders.

'Maybe he's stuck somewhere.'

'What if *you* get stuck?'

'I've got the jeep,' he answered tersely. 'I'll be all right.' Then he stopped beside the door and came back, leaning down to kiss her mouth with a quick stroke. 'You're a good woman, Andy. Keep the fire going, and the coffee hot.'

'And get the wagons in a circle?'

Jason rewarded her comment with a smile and kissed her lightly on the nose. Then he was gone, and a moment later she heard him gun the engine of the jeep before he backed it out into the snowy driveway.

Andrea laid another log in the fireplace and nudged it with the poker until the tongues of flame licked up against it. Where was Robert? she wondered nervously. And where on earth was Jason? It was close to noon now and the snow glistened like diamond sparkles underneath the midday sun. Jason had been gone for close to six hours and she could barely contain the apprehensive thoughts that filled her anxious mind.

She heard a muffled thud in the far end of the house and sat up suddenly. 'Jason?' she called out. 'Is that you?'

'Andrea?' A peevish voice answered. 'Where are you?'

'Robert!' She ran to the kitchen, so relieved to see him that she threw herself into his arms. 'I was worried about you,' she admitted a moment later when she pulled away. 'Oh, look at you!' she exclaimed, dismayed by his wet trousers and ruined shoes. 'You must be frozen. What happened?'

'My car got stuck in a snowdrift,' he answered as she peeled off his overcoat and hung it across a chair. 'I walked the last few miles. Where's Jason?' he demanded. 'Out murdering old ladies?'

'No. He's looking for you,' she answered sharply. 'He's worried about you, too, Robert. Sit down and take your shoes off,' she instructed, coaxing him down to a kitchen chair. 'I'll get you a cup of coffee.'

'Well, he has every reason to be worried,' Robert muttered angrily as he stripped off his sodden shoes and socks. 'Last night I was going to kill him with my bare hands. I still might,' he admitted, shivering with a sudden chill. 'I will if he laid a hand on you. *Did* he lay a hand on you?' he asked her bluntly as she set a cup of coffee beside him on the table.

'No. He's more of a gentleman than you give him credit for,' Andrea reassured him. 'And he didn't know about the will. He didn't,' she repeated firmly when Robert met her eyes with sharp disbelief. 'The money he told you about on the phone is from a business deal he put together months ago. He was completely surprised when I told him about the will.'

'I'll bet he was,' Robert snapped sarcastically. 'Now he has you convinced that he's an innocent victim of misunderstanding, I suppose? Andrea,' he said in an impatiently cold voice. 'Innocent victims don't lie. And they certainly don't kidnap other men's fiancées.'

'I'm not your fiancée,' Andrea pointed out. 'That

was certainly a nice lie you told *him*.'

Robert stiffened at the accusation and at the obvious implication that he was no better than his brother. 'That was different.'

'It certainly was,' she agreed. 'That lie served *your* interests. I'm getting pretty tired of both of you,' she went on before he could make a protest. 'You are both very nice men, and you both deserve part of your father's estate. Don't interrupt me, Robert,' she cautioned when he opened his mouth to disagree. 'You know what decency and fairness and civility are. But you don't bother to extend those to your brother, do you?'

'I've tried.'

'Well, maybe you should try a little harder, because Jason would like to. He hasn't been driving around Maine for the past six hours just because he likes the scenery.'

Andrea had got no further before she was interrupted by the sound of the kitchen door banging shut. 'I'm back, angel!' Jason called out wearily. 'I don't suppose you've heard from . . .' He stopped in the doorway and stared at the man who sat at the kitchen table. 'Robert!' Then his mouth jerked up into a grin. 'I never thought I'd say it, but I'm glad to see you.'

'Oh.' Robert was touched. 'Hello, Jason. Andrea said you were looking for me.'

'Yeah, well . . .' Jason shrugged as he dropped his keys on the table. Then he slid off his parka and tossed it casually on to a nearby chair.

'It was the least I could do under the circumstances. You wouldn't have been out in the storm if it hadn't been for me. Would you like a drink?' he changed the subject suddenly as he strode toward the counter. 'Scotch is what you drink, isn't it?'

'Yes.' Robert slid his hands into his pockets and smiled sheepishly at Andrea. 'Andrea says we should talk, and I suppose we should. We *are* brothers, and it's not necessary to argue over Father's will.'

'I agree,' Jason answered, placing a Scotch and soda in Robert's hands and then leaning down to give Andrea a glass of wine.

'Or over Andrea,' Robert continued with more stiffness, noting Jason's hand as it lingered casually against her shoulder. 'Father meant her to marry me.'

'Father's dead,' Jason reminded him, returning to the counter to pour himself a drink. 'And even if he weren't, slavery is *passé*. I'm surprised you haven't heard the news.'

'I think that's enough,' cautioned Andrea, but neither man was listening.

'What does that mean?' Robert demanded angrily.

'It means that you can't inherit Andy like a piece of family silver,' returned Jason. 'The lady happens to have a mind of her own, and she prefers me.'

'Because you've brainwashed her!' Robert shot back the accusation. 'What kind of man would kidnap my fiancée?'

'What kind of man would kidnap mine?'

'I wish you both would stop!' Andrea exclaimed. Why couldn't they be civil for five minutes? 'I don't want this kind of competition between the two of you!'

'She's mine!' Robert insisted angrily. 'Father intended us to marry, and that's exactly what we're going to do. Andrea can see through your phoney interest. Can't you, Andrea?' She didn't get a chance to answer.

'What is it you *really* want, Robert?' Jason asked his brother pointedly. 'If you want the inheritance, you can bloody well have it. *You* live with oranges and grapefruits for the rest of your life, because I certainly don't intend to.'

'Hah!'

'Hah, yourself!' Jason snapped back angrily. 'You never believed anything I said. You're just like the old man, except you don't have half the guts he had.'

'That's rich,' Robert sneered. 'Coming from a no-account tramp I'm ashamed to call my brother!'

Their conversation had deteriorated to a childish fight, Andrea realised as she closed her eyes and tried to hold back her own rising fury. Neither one wanted her enough to concern himself with how she felt about their bickering. They wanted only to wound each other in a sibling rivalry gone mad.

'I'm *not* a tramp,' Jason answered in a lowered voice that was a warning to back off.

'*I* never disgraced the family name.'

'You wouldn't know how to,' Jason muttered cynically as he pulled open a kitchen drawer and took out a pad of paper. 'I'm going to sign away my rights to the company,' he said in a lower, far more patient voice. 'As a matter of fact, I'm going to give you the whole shooting match—the house, the cars, the stocks, the brandy in the wine cellars. I'm only going to take one thing from the inheritance.'

'What?' Robert asked suspiciously.

Jason nodded his head in Andrea's direction. 'I want her.'

It was an incredible gesture that stopped Robert for a moment. Then he stared at Jason with renewed suspicion. 'This is a trick, isn't it? You're trying to convince Andrea that you really love her, so she'll marry you.'

'You're finally catching on,' Jason answered, finding a pen in the top drawer. 'How does this have to read, Robert? You're the lawyer in the family.'

'It's a bluff. You'll never sign it.'

'Date?' asked Jason, scrawling a date across the top. 'To Whom It May Concern,' he continued with the writing, 'I, Jason Creighton Dorning, suffering no coercion and understanding fully what I write, do hereby promise to give my brother Robert Harrison Dorning all properties, real and otherwise, which I might gain by virtue of my marriage to Andrea . . . What's your middle name, Andy?' he demanded.

'Sarah.'

'Andrea Sarah McKinley,' he continued writing, 'Signed, Jason Creighton Dorning. Does it need a witness?'

'You're out of your mind,' Robert muttered

stiffly. 'If you think this little charade of yours is going to fool Andrea, you're sadly . . .'

'A witness wouldn't hurt,' Jason cut him off as he laid the paper and the pen in front of Andrea. 'Sign your name under mine.'

He was giving away eighty-three million dollars in exchange for her! Andrea stared down at the paper in numb disbelief. Or maybe he was making a gesture, just as Robert suspected, taking a grand risk to convince her that he really loved her. If she signed her name, he would find a way not to hand the paper over to his brother.

There was one way to prove that theory. She wrote her name neatly under Jason's and added the date before she handed the paper back.

'Signed, witnessed, and . . .' Jason's mouth moved outward in a challenging smile as he held the paper out to Robert, '. . . delivered. It's not disappearing ink, in case you're going to accuse me of that old trick.'

'No, I . . .' Robert took the paper and stared at it incredulously. 'This is legal, you know. I'll own everything.'

'Everything but Andy,' Jason reminded him. 'Andy stays with me.'

Like a piece of property, she thought, irritated by the presumption in his voice. She wondered if either brother understood just how insulting that presumption was.

'This is a trick,' Robert repeated peevishly, holding out his hand for Andrea. 'Come along, Andrea. We're going home.'

'Sit right where you are, cupcake,' Jason ordered, extending his arm to keep her in the chair. 'I just gave up eighty-three million dollars to have you. You're not walking out of that door.'

'You're serious about this?' Robert asked. He stared down at the paper for a long moment before he crumpled it and tossed it to the floor. 'You can't have Andrea,' he decided. 'I want her, too.'

'What?' It was Jason's turn to be surprised.

'I said I want her,' Robert repeated firmly. 'She's mine, and I won't let you have her.'

Jason stared at his brother with what seemed like a newly born respect. 'You want her?' he asked bluntly. 'Meaning you love her?'

'Yes,' whispered Robert, glancing restlessly away. 'I love her.'

'Well, I'll be damned,' Jason muttered. 'Watch my brother turn into a human being before your very eyes. Nicely done, Robert,' he complimented in a voice that contained little of his usual sarcastic bite. 'I like you when you admit you have the same feelings that everybody else has.'

'Will you come with me, Andrea?' Robert asked her earnestly.

'Not so quickly!' Jason laid a cautioning hand against her shoulder. 'How much do you love her?'

'How much?' Robert was at a loss to answer.

'Is she worth eighty-three million dollars to you?'

'Oh.'

'Use my paper,' Jason offered, handing him the pad. 'You can use my wording, too. I think I put it rather nicely.'

'That inheritance is mine.'

'He was *my* father, too.' Jason snapped his answer. 'And I'll give you a fat news bulletin, dear brother. I love that woman over there. I'd die for her if I had to.'

But he wouldn't stop quibbling with his brother. They both might love her, but there were too many other emotions that kept getting in the way of love. Andrea sighed wearily and took a sip of wine. Since no one wanted her opinion, she decided not to give it.

'So would I,' Robert answered sharply. 'Maybe I can't put my feelings into words as glibly as you can, but I don't love her any less. Give me the paper.'

Andrea stared at the two men incredulously. She had expected the audacity of Jason's gesture, but it was inconceivable that Robert would give up the company for her.

'Good boy,' Jason said approvingly, putting his arm around his brother's shoulders. 'Now we're getting somewhere. I think we're on the brink of an honest dialogue.'

'I think you're full of yourself!' Robert snapped as he scrawled out his promise to turn the inheritance over to his brother in return for Andrea McKinley's hand.

Jason watched across his shoulder. 'Very nice touch there with the whereases, Robert,' he encouraged. 'Your legal training certainly hasn't been wasted, has it? Now, if the fair lady would sign her name.' He took the pen and paper to Andrea and set it on the table. 'We'll both know what the other is made of.'

'We can throw this one away,' Robert suggested, retrieving Jason's paper from the floor.

'Not so fast, big brother.' Jason took the crumpled sheet of paper out of Robert's hand and smoothed it against the counter top with his hand. 'We've proven that we both love Andy enough to give up father's fortune, but we haven't settled which one of us is going to win the prize. I suggest that we let the lady choose the winner.'

'All right,' Robert answered warily. 'I suppose that's only fair.'

'Here you go, Andy,' Jason said, placing the second, crumpled paper on her lap. 'All you have to do is rip up the one that doesn't apply. But,' he leaned over her and lowered his voice to a low, seductive whisper, 'I'd advise you to take your time. Think about the man you'd like to be with for the rest of your life. The man who could make you feel like a real wo . . .'

'Hey!' Robert objected furiously. 'You didn't say you were going to make a summation to the jury. If you are, I'm going to demand equal time.'

They couldn't stop it for a minute, Andrea thought, staring down at the two papers on her lap. Every moment of conciliation evaporated into discord, and it would always be that way. It would be far worse if she chose one of them above the other.

She loved Jason Dorning, but how could she choose him now that she knew how much Robert Dorning loved her? Refusing him would be the same as telling him he wasn't man enough for her. She cared for him too much to be that cruel.

'Just tear up the one that doesn't apply,' Jason prompted when she didn't move. 'You're the only one who can break this deadlock.'

No one could break their deadlock, she thought wearily. What they were doing now had more to do with family rivalry than love, and maybe it was time they learned that. She put the two sheets together and ripped them both in half.

'What are you doing?' Robert cried incredulously as she turned the pieces and ripped them in half again.

'I wouldn't have either of you on a silver platter,' said Andrea, laying the shredded paper on the table and taking the keys before she strode away.

'But you have to marry one of us!' Robert protested as he pursued her to the door.

'Why?'

'Because . . . we both love you!'

'Robert's right,' Jason agreed matter-of-factly. 'If I can't have you, at least you should marry Robert because . . . because he's a Dorning.'

'That's right,' Robert echoed. 'I'm a Dorning.'

'And so am I!' Jason responded hotly. 'Let's not forget that.'

'I'm not likely to forget,' muttered Andrea, climbing into Jason's jeep and backing it into the driveway. She had had enough of the impossible Dorning family to last her a full lifetime. 'I'll leave your jeep at the airport with the keys above the visor.'

'How am I supposed to get it?' Jason asked as he loped along beside the jeep.

'Walk!'

With that last word she gunned the engine and tore off along the rutted country road.

CHAPTER ELEVEN

ANDREA didn't know what she expected the two Dorning men to do when she roared off in Jason's jeep, but she had expected her decision to end her own confusion. If she couldn't choose between them, then choosing to have neither should have brought her peace of mind at least.

She hadn't expected the image of Jason's face to linger in her mind or the echo of his quicksilver laugh to reverberate through her restless dreams until she was torn apart with longing. Nor had she expected him to give up so completely. He had pursued her so relentlessly she had expected him to appear again to sweep her off her feet, but she seemed to have burned that particular bridge behind her.

She had burned a number of bridges behind her, she thought, sorting through her books to see what she would save and what would be given to the church for its spring rummage sale. Robert hadn't called her. But the most disquieting change was the realisation that she couldn't simply pick up her life again and pretend that Jason Dorning had never made his way into her heart.

Jason had opened a window in her life through which she had seen a vision of herself as a violet-eyed, wild gypsy dancing on exotic shores. She no

longer had Jason's love, but she couldn't shake the
vision of herself that served to make the grey and
chilly city far too confining a place.

'Fitzgerald ... Hemingway ... Agee ... Ir-
ving ...' she murmured as she sorted through her
books, lingering only briefly on her favourites
before she resolutely set them in the box for St
Mary's Church. What was the good of lugging
novels with her half way around the earth? The only
exception she allowed herself was Joseph Dalton's
Farther Now From Home.

'Jarvis Drew ...' She forced herself to concentrate on the task at hand. 'Jarvis Drew?' She stared
at the stack of books with their lurid, tasteless
covers, realising that they were Jason's. They were
the books his father had bequeathed him as an
example of good writing, but Jason hadn't wanted
them.

She certainly didn't, either. She put those in the
box as well, trying to remember how long it had
been since Creighton Dorning died. Two months,
she realised with a start. It seemed like years now
since the day they had gathered for the will.

'Nice of you to give the man a chance ...' It was
Jason's voice that echoed in her mind, sarcastically
amused that she could dismiss Jarvis Drew's
writing after reading only half a page. He was right,
of course. She had been too quick to draw
conclusions, about Jarvis Drew and Jason Dorning,
and about herself as well.

She took out the book on top, studying the cover
illustration of an overblown blonde temptress lying

in a luridly vivid pool of scarlet blood. She slogged through the first two pages before she wrinkled her nose up in disgust and tossed the book back into the box with all the others. 'So much for giving Jarvis Drew a chance,' she muttered, closing up the box and turning to the kitchen.

She was halfway through the cabinets when the doorbell rang, and for one short moment her heart stopped. It wasn't him, she knew, but that realisation didn't stop her hopes from soaring as she made her way around the jumbled boxes to open her front door.

'Hi.' Robert smiled a little sheepishly as he met her blue-eyed stare, then glanced past her to the chaos of her apartment. 'I heard that you were moving, so I thought you might need these.' He gestured to the suitcases on the floor beside him. 'I went to Maine and got them.'

'Oh.' She had hoped that Jason would return them, but she wasn't altogether surprised that it was Robert who had thought of the courtesy. 'Yes, I can use them. Come in.' She stepped back and ushered him inside with a warm smile. Jason was the man she loved, but she had missed Robert, too. If nothing more, they had been friends.

'Where are you going?' asked Robert, concerned.

'I'm not sure.' Andrea tried to make the answer sound less ridiculous than it must seem. 'I'll probably head south. The Bahamas for the winter, the Yucatán, maybe South America . . .'

'What will you do?' He stared at her appalled.

'A little of this, a little of that,' she shrugged. 'I

had a very expensive education,' she reminded him.
'I can type, make coffee, and speak three languages.
What else does a girl need? Speaking of coffee, I
could make some now,' she changed the subject
abruptly just as he opened his mouth to give an
answer. She didn't delude herself that Robert would
approve, but she didn't need anyone's approval any
more. It was *her* life, she had decided, and she was
going to live it. Jason had left her with that resolve,
at least.

'Okay,' he agreed, removing a stack of magazines
from a chair and pulling it up to the kitchen
counter. 'I'll have a cup of coffee.'

'It'll have to be instant,' she apologised, filling the
kettle and setting it on the hob. 'I've already given
away my percolator,' she continued, too aware of
Robert's assessing eyes. Had he come to ask her to
change her mind and marry him after all? she
wondered, afraid that she was going to hurt him one
last time before she went away.

'Are we still friends, Andrea?' Robert asked her
quietly.

'Yes.' There were tears in her eyes and she turned
away, pretending to be concerned with measuring
out the coffee. 'We always will be.'

'I'd like to think so.'

The kettle whistled on the hob and Andrea
removed it to pour two cups of coffee. Then she
pulled up a chair and joined him at the kitchen
counter.

'It's very nice of you to get my suitcases back,' she
thanked him as she sipped her coffee. 'I called

Jason's house several times to ask him to ship them to me, but I never got an answer. I don't suppose . . .' She forced her voice to an even, casual tone that would not betray her feelings. 'I don't suppose you know where he has been?'

'Yes, as a matter of fact,' Robert answered with an unexpectedly wry grimace. 'We went to Israel together.'

'Israel?' Of all the things she expected him to say, that was certainly the last.

'It's a strange story,' he admitted sheepishly. 'Which has to do with oranges and being too drunk to say no to Jason's bright ideas. You know how he can be. His enthusiasm can be a little too infectious sometimes.'

'Israel?' Andrea repeated incredulously.

'Yeah, well . . .' For a moment she could hear Jason's speech mannerisms in Robert's embarrassed explanation. 'It was there and we weren't. After you left the house, we got pretty drunk.

'We talked, and we cried into our beers. Jason kept saying, "We've done it now, Robert. We tore our pretty toy in two by fighting over it like stupid asses." Then he decided that we didn't need you. "We're *Dornings*!" he said. "What do we need with a silly girl who can't make up her mind?" He was angry, of course. That's why he talked like that.'

'*Then* you went to Israel?'

'Er . . . no, then we went to Montreal. Because, you see, it . . . er . . . was there and we weren't.'

'Of course.' Andrea pursed her lips together to hold back a smile. Robert was having a hard enough time telling her the story. It probably wouldn't help if she burst into a laugh.

'He decided to show me his favourite bar. So, there we were in Jason's favourite bar, and then in another one of Jason's favourite bars, and in another one ... And I happened to mention casually that they grow oranges in Israel. So, of course, we flew to Tel Aviv. By that time Jason had started to sober up, and he had acquired a typewriter and a tape recorder from somewhere and he was following me around asking me questions about oranges.

'I managed to conduct some business while we were there,' Robert confessed. 'And Jason banged out the first six chapters of his book.'

'His book?' Andrea prompted curiously. 'Jason's writing a book about *oranges*?'

'Hm. He showed up at the house last night and asked me for my opinion,' Robert leaned forward to confide. 'It's about me and father and oranges and God knows what else, and it's really quite moving. I told Jason I had no idea he had that much talent.'

Andrea stared at Robert in amazement. Their escapade in Israel paled beside the notion that Jason would ask Robert for an opinion on his writing and that Robert would respond with open praise. It seemed that the world had tumbled upside down in the space of one short month.

Robert frowned as he tapped his fingernails against the polished surface of the counter. 'He showed me something else that he had written,' he went on in a low, troubled voice. 'He gave me a document that signed away all rights to Father's estate, and he said it was a wedding present to you. He said . . .' He stopped and took a breath. 'He said that since everything would be mine anyway, you'd know I was marrying you for love.'

'I can't marry you, Robert,' she said regretfully.

'I expected you to say that,' Robert admitted as he reached out and took her trembling hand in his. 'But I came here to propose, so I'd like to finish. If I can't have you, I won't stand in the way of your marrying the man you love. Would you marry Jason if he asked you, Andrea?'

'Yes.' Her answer was a whisper.

'I thought you might,' Robert smiled with bittersweet affection. 'Well,' he murmured as he stroked her knuckles lightly with his thumb, 'I'd better get you to the airport, then. He's on his way to Puerto Rico.'

'Puerto Rico?' Andrea was dismayed. 'Because it's there and he's not?'

'No,' he corrected. 'Because it's there and *you're* not.'

The plane was gone.

Andrea stared up at the television that was bolted to the wall, reading the dismal truth in the figures they displayed. Planes were forever being delayed at Logan Airport, but this once the plane had left on schedule, tearing Jason from her grasp too soon.

She stared at the schedule until the words blurred before her eyes. Then she took a breath and squared her shoulders stubbornly as she turned back to the ticket desk.

'When does the next flight leave for Puerto Rico?'

'Puerto Rico?' The ground stewardess consulted the schedule on the counter. 'Tomorrow morning at nine-fifteen.'

Tomorrow? Jason could be anywhere by tomorrow, Andrea thought, trying to smile despite her sense of desperation. 'All right,' she sighed, slipping a credit card out of her wallet. 'I'd like to book a ticket. Coach.'

At least she would have a chance to pack, she thought as she put the ticket in her bag. If she were going to chase Jason Dorning half way around the planet, she might as well have clothes.

Robert had driven her to the airport and had agreed to return to her apartment to pack up what was left, but she could do that now. She would ask Mrs Walters down the hall to pick up her mail and have it forwarded through Robert. What else needed to be done? Andrea wondered as she stopped beside the airport snack bar and searched vainly in her purse for change. Maybe Robert would know who Jason intended to see in Puerto Rico.

She took out a dollar and slid it across the counter. 'Could I have change for the phone, please?' She turned around with the coins clutched in her hand, and stopped. There, at the far end of the room, sat a man she recognised as well as she recognised her own reflection in a mirror. Jason sat, morose and lost in thought, staring at an orange on the table in front of him.

'Where was it grown?' Andrea asked, stopping at the table and smiling as he met her eyes in stunned bewilderment. 'The orange,' she repeated, touching it with her finger until it rolled slowly towards him. 'California? Florida? Poland?'

'I don't think they grow oranges in Poland.' Jason didn't take his eyes away from her. 'I don't know where it was grown.'

'Robert would know,' she suggested as she sat down and placed her bag beside her on the table. 'He knows about pineapples, too. And fruits I've never even seen—loquats and atemoyas. What are you doing here?' she asked conversationally. 'Are you coming or going?'

'I'm not quite sure,' he murmured, dropping his gaze before the relentlessness of her blue-eyed stare. He had been here in plenty of time to catch the plane, Andrea guessed, glancing at the ashtray on the table. But he hadn't gone. 'What are *you* doing here?' Jason countered in an effort to change the subject. 'If you came to have lunch, it's not the greatest restaurant in Boston.'

'I came to buy a plane ticket. I'm going on a honeymoon.'

'Oh.' Pain flickered across his handsome face and then disappeared as he made an effort to smile civilly. 'Congratulations. Robert said he was going to propose to you.'

'He did,' said Andrea as she picked up the orange and made a show of sniffing the stem end. 'I suppose I'll have to learn something about oranges if I'm going to share my husband's interests. I think that's important, don't you?'

'Yes,' he glanced restlessly away, and his jaw tensed with a new hardness, 'I suppose it is.'

'And patience will be important, too,' she continued evenly. 'I don't think marriage to a Dorning could ever be easy.'

'He's not a bad sort,' Jason muttered in his brother's defence. 'He's actually . . . he's decent, and he's . . . er . . . he loves you very much,' he continued gamely although the effort to appear disinterested was tearing him apart. 'He could be more romantic if he tried. If a man loves a woman enough, he tries to be what she wants him to be . . .'

'Do you think it's possible for a man to change?' she asked curiously, doubting that notion a great deal. She was in love with an exasperating, erratic man. She might as well resign herself to that. 'Especially a Dorning? I've always thought that the Dornings were a bit more stubborn than the ordinary man. I hope I'm woman enough to make my husband happy.'

'You are,' he reassured her tersely. 'Any man would be lucky to have you, Andy.'

'Thank you.' Andrea found a penknife in her purse and slit the orange open. 'Your opinion means a lot to me, Jason. It always has, and I imagine it will mean even more when I'm your wife.'

His eyes met hers with so much bewildered consternation that she almost laughed out loud.

'What did you say?' he demanded in a breathless whisper.

'I said your opinion means a lot to me.' She deliberately misunderstood his question. She gave him a coquettish smile as she divided the orange into two equal halves. 'What do you think of Puerto Rico for a honeymoon? I've never been there, so I don't know what it's like, but I already have a ticket.'

'Do you?' Jason's mouth curved upward in a long, slow smile of understanding. 'I suppose we shouldn't waste it.'

'No, I don't suppose we should.' She put an orange section between her lips and sucked it gently to extract the juice, knowing full well how seductive she was being with her deliberate casualness. Jason's eyes glowed with amused delight.

'Are you going to propose to me?' she asked matter-of-factly. 'Or is it my turn to propose to you? I've lost track.'

Jason didn't answer immediately. He leaned forward and balanced his chin against his knuckles to study her flushed, smiling face. The eyes that lingered on her features were so rich with devotion that Andrea lost herself for a long moment in those warm, brown pools of light, feeling her life open all around her with the promise of excitement. Life with Jason Dorning would be exasperating, but it would not be dull.

'Marry me, Andrea McKinley?' Jason asked in a throaty whisper that was far more serious than she expected. His long fingers curled around hers with an insistent touch. 'I've loved you since the birth of time, and I'll go on loving you until eternity has passed into oblivion.'

'Well . . .' She was breathlessly pleased with the romantic words, and by the earnestness with which he had said them.

Jason met her eyes with a self-mocking smile. 'Is that long enough for you, cupcake? Or do you want something a little more permanent?'

'Don't!' she snapped impatiently, pressing her thumb against his lips. 'Don't you dare spoil this moment with a joke, Jason Dorning!' She glanced around her, aware of the attention they were attracting from the people at the other tables in the snack bar, but Jason didn't notice them at all.

'It wasn't a joke, angel,' he said softly as he pressed his lips caressingly against the softness of her palm. 'My love for you never was.'

CHAPTER TWELVE

'I'm home, and I'm hungry!' Jason's voiced boomed out from the hallway. Then, before Andrea could answer, he was in the kitchen, filling that spacious, sunlit room with the masculine energy of his presence.

'Good. I've made us lunch.'

'It's not food I want,' Jason answered as he caught her in his strong arms and lifted her completely off her feet in an enthusiastic greeting.

'And what *do* you want, you barbarian?' she laughed as she circled his broad shoulders with her arms. A month of marriage had done nothing to diminish the intensity of their passion. If anything, their love had grown more boundless with every passing day.

'I want you,' he whispered as his mouth met hers in a teasingly light kiss. Then his mouth descended once again with a greedy hunger that demanded a submission she was glad to give.

Their embrace filled an immeasurable span of moments that might have been eternity or only the length of a heartbeat's fluttering life. Andrea didn't know. She only knew that she was filled with a contentment that drove all other thoughts away. This man had always been her fate. Now he was her present and her future and all of life itself.

'I adore you, angel,' Jason whispered as his mouth lingered on her cheek. 'You know that, don't you?'

'I had guessed,' she admitted teasingly, still clinging to his shoulders. 'Besides, you told me yesterday, remember? If you're not careful, you're going to spoil me.'

'Do you adore *me*?' he demanded.

'Mm-hm.'

'Do you *really* adore me?'

'Yes, I really . . .' Andrea stopped to study her husband's flushed face and sparkling eyes. He had gone into town to run errands and pick up the mail, but he'd returned with a look she recognised too well. It was his cat-with-a-canary expression. 'What's rolling around in that convoluted mind of yours, Jason?' she asked warily, wondering what mischief he had been up to in the past few hours.

'I got you a present while I was in town.'

'Not more oranges?' she groaned. She had seen far too many oranges on their month-long honeymoon in the Caribbean. Even now, home in Maine with Jason working on his book, the house was filled with fruit; whatever Robert thought might pique his brother's interest.

'No oranges.'

'Or orange juice, or candied orange peel, or orange perfume, or . . .'

'It's something you'll like,' Jason promised, dumping the satchel that contained the mail on the kitchen table and pushing a square package across the polished surface. 'Open it,' he ordered. 'I've been waiting for a month to give you this surprise.'

Andrea tore off the wrapping and stared at the book she found inside. '*The Beggar's Bargain*,' she read from the cover. 'It's a new Joseph Dalton novel!'

'Read the dedication.'

'The dedication?' Andrea opened the book and read the words that were centred on the page. ' "To the violet-eyed gypsy I adore." What an odd coincidence. He's used the same words you use to describe . . .' She stopped. Jason's grin had spread until it nearly split his face, and any moment he would be laughing.

Andrea stared at him, then at the book, and understanding pierced at last. 'You're him?' She pointed to the cover of the book. 'I'm married to Joseph Dalton?'

'Yep.' Jason made a show of casual uninterest. 'That's the good news. Bill, bill, advertisement,' he murmured as he sorted through the mail.

'What's the bad news?' Andrea demanded, studying her husband with renewed suspicion. He still had a secret. That was clear enough from the way his eyes evaded her relentless, blue-eyed stare. Knowing Jason, the secret could be anything.

'Do you remember that misunderstanding about the money I was going to come into? You thought it was my father's estate and it was something else entirely?'

'Yes.' Andrea remembered. Jason had told her it was a business deal, but he had never told her any details. 'Has that fallen through?'

'Not exactly. But my agent says it's going to mean publicity—talk shows, magazine articles,' he shrugged. 'I've tried to avoid that in the past, but the network is demanding a public relations clause in the contract for the television series based on my writing.'

'There's going to be a television series?' Andrea asked, bewildered. 'Based on your other book, *Farther Now From Home*?'

'Not exactly.'

'What exactly?' she asked in exasperation. 'Are you trying to drive me out of my mind, Jason?'

'My other books. The . . . er . . . the Jarvis Drew mysteries.'

'You're *Jarvis Drew*, too?'

'Yeah, well.' He gave her a sheepishly apologetic smile. 'There were a few years when no one wanted the great American novel, and I wanted to eat.'

'Jarvis Drew,' she whispered, taking another look at her strange husband. '*Ms* magazine called you a morally degenerate Neanderthal.'

'Hm. "Where others merely flirt with the dark underbelly of depravity, Jarvis Drew slits it open for an inspection of the entrails." His mouth twitched outward into a mischievous smile as he quoted a review he obviously enjoyed. '*New York Times Review of Books*,' he added with a grin. 'I've always liked that one.

'There's a letter from Robert here,' he changed the subject as he returned his attention to the mail. 'Did I tell you that he's offered us thirty per cent of his shares in Dorning Import with the provision that he retain the voting proxy?'

'Jarvis Drew!' Andrea repeated in a whisper as she leaned back against the kitchen counter. 'I suppose I'll have to read those books now!'

'And you've got another package,' he announced, holding a manila envelope up to the light. 'No doubt diamonds from an ardent admirer. You don't have anything going with Vincent Carpezzi, do you?' he asked, squinting to read the return address.

'Why didn't you tell me about your books?'

'I wanted to surprise you with the dedication. And I thought it would be best if you knew I was Joseph Dalton before you found out that I was Jarvis Drew,' Jason admitted honestly. 'Can I open this, cupcake?'

'Sure,' she answered distractedly, opening the book she still held in her hand to re-read the romantic dedication. Then she turned the page and started to read Jason's novel.

He slit the envelope open and dumped a letter and a videotape sealed in a package on the kitchen table. ' "Dear Andrea," ' he read the note aloud. ' "It is with some hesitation that I send you the enclosed videotape. My instructions were to give it to Mr and Mrs Dorning on the occasion of their marriage. Creighton Dorning obviously meant it to be viewed by Mr and Mrs *Robert* Dorning, not by Mr and Mrs *Jason* Dorning. The container is sealed, and I was instructed not to view it myself." '

"You can understand my present dilemma. The Dorning family has so recently repaired its wounds, I do not wish to be party to an unfortunate rekindling of old arguments. I suggest that you view the tape yourself and use your wisdom and compassion to make a proper disposition. Your faithful servant, Vincent Carpezzi."

'God only knows what Father said,' Jason agreed, picking up the container and slitting it open with his knife to remove the tape. 'Let's see what he had to say.'

'I should probably watch it alone first,' Andrea suggested, but she was too late to stop him. Jason had left the room and was already at the stairs. Andrea quickly followed. 'I should probably watch it alone,' she repeated at the doorway of their bedroom. 'That's what Mr Carpezzi suggested.'

'What could he have said, angel?' Jason asked impatiently. 'He's going to tell you that he arranged a competition for your hand, and then he's going to congratulate you on your marriage to my brother. Sit down on the bed,' he ordered. Then his face softened into a challenging smile as his eyes flickered to her disapproving face. 'Unless you don't want to be in bed with Jarvis Drew.'

'I'd rather be in bed with Joseph Dalton.'

'That can be arranged,' he promised as he pushed the tape into the slot and pushed a button to bring the screen to life. Then he seized her wrist and coaxed her to the bed, meeting her mouth with a quick kiss as he stretched himself beside her.

'Hello, you two.' The white-haired man on the screen smiled fondly as he poured himself a glass of brandy. 'I am a bit inebriated at the moment, so you'll have to forgive me if I ramble. I've been sitting here thinking about my life and what I would have liked to have done with it if I had had more time. I would have liked to drink a toast at your wedding.

'To two of my favourite people.' He lifted his glass high. 'To Andrea and to my son. You've got yourself a good husband, Andrea,' Creighton admitted as he took a sip. 'Oh, I've complained about my sons in the past, but the truth is that both of them are good men. Robert is intelligent and hard-working. So is Jason, for that matter. Or Jarvis or Joseph, or whatever else he's calling himself these days. He said he didn't want to use the Dorning name, and given the nature of some of his books, I think I owe him a debt of gratitude. Not that I didn't read them. Not that I didn't like them, too,' he added with a chuckle of amusement. 'My favourite was *Hand From the Grave*. I was thinking of that book when I made my will.'

'You were right,' Andrea admitted as she relaxed beside her husband and laid her cheek against the hollow of his shoulder. 'It was all a plot to make Robert jealous.'

'I know that Jason will see the obvious loophole in the will,' the old man explained with a smile of satisfaction as he leaned back against the cushions of his chair. 'I expect he'll give Robert a good run for his money, and that Robert will rise to the occasion. I don't think Robert will lose the business to his brother, but I think he'll sweat a little over the possibility. Maybe the two of them will learn to respect each other into the bargain. That's my greatest hope. My second greatest hope is to see Andrea married to my son.'

'I wonder what he'd say if he knew what happened,' Andrea murmured as she kissed Jason's neck and let her mouth linger there against his fragrant skin. 'He'd probably be appalled that I married the family barbarian.'

'No doubt.' Jason rewarded her comment with a grin. He turned his head against the pillow until his mouth brushed hers in a seductively light kiss. Then his lips touched her mouth again, lingering there until she softened with desire.

'Be a good wife to my son, Andrea.' Creighton Dorning's voice rolled over them like a benediction. 'And you tell Jason to be good to you.'

Jason stiffened in Andrea's embrace, then he pulled away to stare at his father's image on the screen. Andrea stared, too. Creighton Dorning had been arrogant enough to think that life would go exactly as he had planned it. And he had been absolutely right. 'I'll be damned!' Jason let out a gust of breath. 'The old goat outsmarted me.'

'Better yet, *don't* tell him to be good to you,' Creighton advised with an impish twinkle in his eyes. 'That boy never listened to his father.

'To you.' He lifted his brandy glass in one last smiling toast. 'You were meant for one another.'

For the millions who can't read
Give the Gift of Literacy

One out of five adults in North America
cannot read or write well enough
to fill out a job application
or understand the directions on a bottle of medicine.

**You can change all this by joining the fight
against illiteracy.**

For more information write to:
Contact, Box 81826, Lincoln, Neb. 68501
In the United States, call toll free: 800-228-3225

**The only degree you need
is a degree of caring**

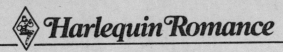
Harlequin Romance

Coming Next Month

2845 WHEN LOVE FLIES BY Jeanne Allen
The strong sensitive man sitting beside a frightened American admires her for facing her fear of flying. But Lindsey has a greater fear—that of loving a man who, like her late father, makes a living flying planes.

2846 TEMPERED BY FIRE Emma Goldrick
She's a young doctor, planning a quiet summer of convalescence. He's an ex-military man, now writing a book and planning a peaceful summer of work. They meet in New England—and all plans for peace and quiet go up in flames!

2847 FUSION Rowan Kirby
Despite her successful career, a solicitor, whose husband deserted her and their son, feels so emotionally insecure that she struggles against getting involved again, even when she finds a man she could love.

2848 IN LOVE WITH THE MAN Marjorie Lewty
Delighted to be part of a fact-finding team of Tokyo, a computer operator's pleasure is spoiled when her big boss unexpectedly accompanies them and thinks she's an industrial spy.

2849 STAIRWAY TO DESTINY Miriam MacGregor
Delcie, a typist, tired of catering to the need of her overprotective aunts, decides to work for a renowned New Zealand author at his sheep station. There she learns about her own needs . . . as a woman.

2850 BEYOND HER CONTROL Jessica Steele
Brooke rushes to France to rescue her young sister from a case of puppy love for a worldly, wealthy chateau owner—only to fall in love with him herself!

Available in July wherever paperback books are sold, or through Harlequin Reader Service.

In the U.S.
901 Fuhrmann Blvd.
P.O. Box 1397
Buffalo, N.Y. 14240-1397

In Canada
P.O. Box 603
Fort Erie, Ontario
L2A 5X3

Take 4 best-selling love stories FREE
Plus get a FREE surprise gift!

ATTRACTIVE, SPACE SAVING BOOK RACK

Display your most prized novels on this handsome and sturdy book rack. The hand-rubbed walnut finish will blend into your library decor with quiet elegance, providing a practical organizer for your favorite hard-or soft-covered books.

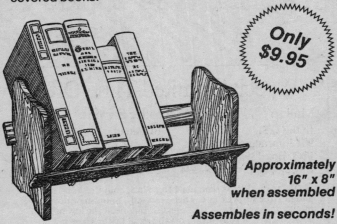

Only $9.95

Approximately 16" x 8" when assembled

Assembles in seconds!

To order, rush your name, address and zip code, along with a check or money order for $10.70* ($9.95 plus 75¢ postage and handling) payable to *Harlequin Reader Service*:

JULIE ELLIS

author of the bestselling
Rich Is Best rivals the likes of
Judith Krantz and Belva Plain with

THE ONLY SIN

It sweeps through the glamorous cities of Paris, London, New York and Hollywood. It captures life at the turn of the century and moves to the present day. *The Only Sin* is the triumphant story of Lilli Landau's rise to power, wealth and international fame in the sensational fast-paced world of cosmetics.